HOME TO WITCHEND

Mary grabbed Dickie's arm and pointed at the hill in front of them.

"Look!" she gasped. "There's a man up there – he's shouting. Something's wrong..."

Suddenly, with a thunderous roar, the hill burst open, and a great wave of brown water surged down towards them...

But as the twins face terror in Harkaway Hollow, David and Peter are heading into even greater danger – for they have met the Lone Piners' old enemy, the evil Miss Ballinger. And when David sets out to follow her trail, he fails to return...

Also by Malcolm Saville and in Jade Paperbacks

Sea Witch Comes Home

HOME TO WITCHEND

A Lone Pine Story

MALCOLM SAVILLE

Jade Publishers
Haslemere

Jade Publishers
15 Stoatley Rise
Haslemere
Surrey GU27 1AF

First published 1978
First published in Jade Paperbacks 1990

© Copyright the Estate of Malcom Saville 1978, 1990
Cover design © Jade Publishers 1990

All rights reserved. No part of this publication may be reproduced, stored in a retrieval system, or transmitted in any form or by any means, electronic, mechanical photocopying, recording or otherwise without the prior written permission of the publishers. The book is sold subject to the condition that it shall not, by way of trade or otherwise be lent, re-sold, hired out or otherwise circulated without the publisher's prior consent in any form of binding or cover other than that in whch it is published and without a similar condition including this condition being imposed on the subsequent purchaser.

Cover illustration by Ron King
Cover design by Samantha Edwards

Computer typeset by 'Keyword', Tring, Herts
Printed and bound by Cox & Wyman, Reading, Berks

British Library Cataloguing in Publication Data
Saville, Malcolm *1901–1982*
Home to witchend
I. Title
823.912 [J]

ISBN 0-903461-37-4

CONTENTS

Page

    Foreword 7

1. Easy Money 13
2. Peter's Dream 22
3. The *Gay Dolphin* 35
4. Enter the Twins 47
5. Appledore 61
6. Disaster 73
7. "Call Me Tim" 91
8. David and Peter Go Shopping 103
9. Enter Mr Cantor 113
10. Not So Clever 126
11. Peter to the Rescue 140
12. Home to Witchend 152
    Appendix 169

To all Lone Piners of all ages everywhere. With gratitude for their loyalty through so many years.

FOREWORD

This is the twentieth story about a group of boys and girls who founded a secret club at an old house called Witchend in a remote valley in the Shropshire hills. The site of their first camp was marked by a solitary pine tree high on the bank above the house, and so they called their club after the tree. Now they are known as the Lone Piners in many parts of the world.

The first story of their adventures was called *Mystery at Witchend*. Since then, many boys and girls have formed their own Lone Pine Clubs, and have tried to keep the simple rules of the first Lone Piners, the most important of which is, *"To be true to each other whatever happens always."*

Many readers have asked me if the original characters ever existed, or whether they are based on any boys and girls I have known. They are not, and neither are the adults featured in any of the stories. They are all imaginary and have no reference to any living person, although some of them have become very real to me during the years I have been writing about them.

During this time some readers have asked that all the Lone Piners should remain the same age as they were in the first story. Others have wanted them all to get older with each book, but if I had done that, the four eldest would now be well into middle age, so neither of these suggestions was possible. But some changes were essential in a series spanning so many years, so now the three older couples have left school and are about eighteen. They have changed, I hope naturally enough, in their attitudes to the times in which they are now living and, as you will see in this story, have become aware of what they really mean to each other, and that is not a bad thing.

I could not allow the irrepressible twins to grow up as quickly as the others, but older readers will soon realize that they could not forever converse in the childish manner which they used in the earlier stories.

Macbeth, the twins' Scottie, is ageing a little but seems to be immortal!

Every Lone Pine adventure is set against a British background which you can explore yourself. This one, like the first, and nine others, takes place in the Shropshire hills. The names I have given to most of the places are imaginary and, although you will not find Witchend, Ingles Farm or the bigger house and farm called Seven White Gates, you can visit and climb the magnificent mountain called the Long Mynd and the sinister Stiperstones a few miles nearer Wales. This is all unforgettable and unspoiled country, and the best centre from which to explore it is the little town of Church Stretton, on the main road from Shrewsbury to Ludlow.

I have many friends, old and young, to thank for their interest and help in planning this particular story. Over the years, hundreds of readers have suggested the sort of adventure they would like the twentieth to be. A few early readers who have seen the series through have become my friends and have contributed to the planning of this story.

And of these I am happy to acknowledge the help given to me by Vivien Turner, one of my earliest and most loyal of fans, who subsequently produced a small Lone Piner of her own. The details of the fictional characters and their relations, friends, and enemies at the end of the book and been compiled by her, and I am grateful.

You may also like to know that the dramatic, natural calamity described in Chapter 6 actually occurred in 1970, and if you can discover the valley you will see the scars of the explosion on the hillside.

The Lone Pine Club

There are nine fictional members of the original club and they all appear in this story.

DAVID MORTON is eighteen. Lives in London and is training to be a solicitor. He is the first and only Captain of the Club. His parents are the owners of Witchend.

RICHARD (DICKIE) and MARY MORTON are David's twin brother and sister. Age nearly twelve.

PETRONELLA (PETER) STERLING has her eighteenth birthday in this story and now works in a riding stable at Ludlow. Has no mother but lives with her retired father at Witchend. Peter is really the founder of the Club after she met the Mortons when they came to Witchend in the first story.

TOM INGLES is about the same age as David. He is an orphaned Londoner, but lives and works at his uncle's farm about half a mile from Witchend. One of the original members of the Club, he is now an enthusiastic working farmer.

JENNY HARMAN is an excitable, attractive redhead who has also left school and now works in a bookshop in Shrewsbury. She lives with her father and stepmother who keep the General Store and Post Office in the village of Barton Beach near the Stiperstones, where she was born. Since her schooldays, Tom Ingles has had no need to remind her, "Don't forget that you're *my* girl." She never has.

JONATHAN (JON) and **PENELOPE (PENNY) WARRENDER** are cousins who have also left school and live in the ancient town of Rye in Sussex. Jon is at Sussex University and Penny, after a domestic science course, is interested in hotel management. At the time of this story she is training at the Gay Dolphin Hotel in Rye, which is jointly owned by her parents and Jon's widowed mother. They have not shared all the Lone Piner's adventures but are very close friends.

HARRIET SPARROW is a special friend of the twins and about the same age. She is a Londoner, too, the latest recruit to the Club, and a great favourite of the others.

CHAPTER 1

Easy Money

The elderly woman, once known to her colleagues – and indeed to the police – as Miss Ballinger, had found it essential to change her names many times.

On the April evening when this story opens she was Mrs Pamela Browning, an eccentric artist who had been recently widowed. A few months ago she had bought a small house in Stella Avenue in a suburb of Birmingham.

It was soon realized that she was the sort of woman who kept herself to herself. Her neighbours were naturally curious when she arrived, but their offers of help were gruffly declined. Later, she let it be known that she was an artist who designed greetings cards and was too busy to make new friends. She lived alone, never seemed to have any visitors and did not use local shops. It was not surprising that she was soon written off as an eccentric and rude old woman.

But on this particular evening, just as dusk was falling, a taxi brought Mrs Browning an attractive young visitor. Inquisitive neighbours would certainly have been surprised and intrigued if they could have heard the conversation between the two women after the curtains were drawn across the windows of the front room.

Mrs Browning was an ugly, thick-set woman of about sixty, with untidy, straggling grey hair. She was often remembered by the heavy, thick-lensed spectacles which she was forced to wear. Another unusual characteristic was a hoarse, deep voice, which she sometimes tried to disguise.

She nearly always dressed carelessly – depending on the sort of person she was pretending to be.

Her companion was about thirty – smart and attractive. More than once she had posed as "Ballinger's niece" and had played nearly as many parts as her "aunt". Her name was Valerie, and now, as she lit another cigarette from the glowing stub of her last, she turned to the older woman.

"Now, Auntie," she said. "Let's get down to business. I want to know why you wanted me in a hurry. What are you up to in this ghastly place?" As no answer to this was forthcoming, she went on, "He warned me that I should be hearing from you. What does he want? And I'll tell you something else, Auntie. You're not looking too well."

The older woman frowned. "I'll thank you to remember that my name is now Pamela Browning and I lost my dear husband only a few months ago. At present it is convenient for me to live quietly in the Midlands where I am employing my skills with reasonable success. I will not ask you how you spend your time, but I presume you are not married to the objectionable young man who caused us so much trouble some years ago?"

"No business of yours what I do with my life," retorted Valerie, "but I got rid of Dale ... What does Grandon want?" she asked again. "I had a note from Brussels saying that I would be wise to come here when you asked me. And here I am, so get on with it. I don't care for this place – or very much for you."

"You will soon change your ideas, Val," replied the Ballinger. "You will *have* to do so. Our old colleague, whose name is now Thomas Seymour, has kept in touch with me. He asked me for your address in London. Now, Val, listen to me carefully. Seymour is a wealthy and important man. He has been living in France and Belgium for some years, and you will be wise to realize that he knows too much about us both and could make things awkward if we don't work with him. He tells me that he has a proposition for us and he is coming here tonight and bringing a friend with him. I understand, Val, that the proposition would be profitable for us if we work with him. Would you care to increase your income – whatever else you may be doing?"

Valerie stubbed out her cigarette.

"Yes, I would. Things aren't too good since I got rid of Les. But what's it all about? I can understand why he might want you to do some of his dirty work, but why *me*? Have you two been arranging something? And who is the mysterious friend? Another woman? Are you sure that he really *is* in the money?"

"I'll tell you what I know, Val. I think he wants you because he knows that if you don't play the fool we can both work well together on the 'Auntie and pretty niece' act, and while we're on that subject – you're not looking as young as you were . . ." The Ballinger's tone became harsh. "No, Val. You can't fool me. I've known you too long. We're both ready for another break. There's not enough cash for me in this artist's business, and you should know me well enough to be sure that I'm always on the lookout for something better. I believe you are too. Do you want to hear me, or do you want me to tell him that you've lost your nerve and gone soft?"

"How do I know you're playing fair with me?" Val objected. "How do I know what you've fixed with Seymour – or whatever he calls himself now?"

"You can't be sure till you know more, Val. I'm willing to tell you all I know and what he's asked me to do. Fact is, we're useful to each other. We know Seymour, too, and if you're sensible and listen to what I say, I don't think he'll make fools of us. He will have to be reminded that we know quite a lot about *him*."

The girl nodded.

"OK, Auntie, dear. Tell me more. What does he want?"

"I know nothing of the friend he's bringing here, but about a month ago Seymour asked me to find an isolated house in a country district somewhere around this part of the Midlands. He told me not to advertise, but to watch the

'Property For Sale' columns in the local papers. The house must be isolated, with some outbuildings and certainly a cellar. It must have electricity and telephone."

"What is he going to do in such a place?"

"I'm not sure, but we'll find out. I've a feeling that he's on to something big – so big that there could be a lot of easy money for both of us if we play our cards right. I've found exactly what he's looking for." The Ballinger paused for a moment. "I sent him the details a week ago and that's why he's coming here in a hurry tonight. And that's why you're here too. I'm convinced that he wouldn't get us together again unless he was on to something big. The man he's bringing is his new partner in France: it could be that he wants us to represent him over here."

"Seymour thinks he's safer the other side of the water, no doubt," Val sneered, "but let's hear what he's got to say. Are you sure he's *really* in the money?"

"We shall soon know . . ." The Ballinger looked up quickly. "I think I heard a car. On the kitchen table is a tray of drinks. Just bring it in as soon as they have settled down."

Valerie stood up and said unpleasantly, "No thanks, Auntie, I'll welcome them both *with* you. We must be sure we're not keeping anything from each other, mustn't we? No little secrets with our rich friends."

Valerie pushed the older woman aside none too gently, and it was as well that she did not see the fury in the Ballinger's face as she stumbled after her "niece" down the narrow hall. The doorbell rang.

It was a long time since either of the women had seen the man who was once known as Grandon, and their first impression in the dusk was that he was now very much more confident of himself. And, as the Ballinger had hinted, his clothes, and the large car now parked outside, suggested that he was certainly in the money. When they had first known him, he wore a little narrow black moustache. Now he was bearded and very well groomed.

He shook hands with them both, but it was not until the front door was closed that he introduced his companion.

"This is my good friend and business partner, Josef," he said. "I have told him that you have both worked with me in the past and that you are discreet and can be trusted."

Josef made no attempt to shake hands, but nodded to the two women and muttered, "Goot evening."

In the stronger light of the sitting room, they saw that in appearance Josef was a marked contrast to his smart companion. He was wearing tinted spectacles which hid his eyes, so it was difficult to guess his age. He was short, stoutish, rather untidy and grubby, and they noticed that the fingers of both hands were stained as if with acid.

"We are ready to talk," the Ballinger said, "but you should understand that both of us must be given full details of your plans and of what our co-operation is worth to you. The past must be forgotten. You know that I am a working artist known as 'Pam' and my full name is now Pamela Browning. Valerie is still known as Val, but, if your terms to us are agreeable, no doubt she can be persuaded to act again as my niece. We must know first what you have to offer . . . We should also like to know more about your colleague. Val, my dear, would you kindly bring in the drinks?"

It was evident that Val was rather obviously interested in the dandified Thomas Seymour. He got up to open the door for her, followed her into the kitchen and returned carrying the tray. Being extremely short-sighted, the Ballinger did not see the warm, friendly smile Val gave him, but she did sense that the girl had soon made up her mind about the chances of easy money.

For the next half-hour, the four ill-assorted people discussed and planned a plot that was daring in its comparative simplicity. Seymour did the talking because the idea was his, and the two women were soon aware that they would have to accept his leadership.

First he explained that Josef was already working with

HOME TO WITCHEND

him in Belgium and France, but that he wanted a bigger workshop and more scope in England.

"Josef is a highly skilled engraver and printer," said Seymour. "He was trained in Germany and we first met five years ago. I want you both to join us in my plan to actually make money. You see, my old friends, we are already *printing* money in Belgium and France, and I intend, with your help and Josef's skill, to print banknotes in England." He paused for a moment, then went on, "I believe that you, Pam, have found a house where Josef can do his printing in secrecy. We will consider the details in a moment, but the property you have found will be bought in *your* name if we decide, after a visit tomorrow, that it is suitable for our purpose. You are an artist in your own right. You have told me that you are designing and selling greetings cards and selling them in country markets, and so, I suggest, it is natural for you to buy a remote house where you can work in peace and quiet and which is not too far from the busy cities of the Midlands."

"And what about *me*?" Val demanded. "Where do I come in? I'm not saying that I won't work this racket, but I don't think you're being very friendly about it. Not like the old days."

"No, Val. It is *not* like the old days," replied Seymour. "I've won through. I've proved that by making false money I can make a lot of easy money. So can you and your aged 'Auntie' here, and I reckon in six months I will have made enough for us all to live wherever we like in another country. In the sunshine . . . We can all forget the past and our struggles. Forget that I was once Grandon and Pam here was Ballinger . . . Josef is with us and together nothing can stop us. Already some of the money he makes is circulating down south in places like Dover and Folkestone and Canterbury. It is there that visitors from France and Holland and Belgium come over every day on the car ferries, to shop in England."

Seymour sipped his drink. "Well!" he continued, "are you two ready to come in with us while the going is good? What about the artistic Miss Ballinger? But I must get used to calling you Pam. Val, of course, has always been Val and must stay that way . . . Josef is just Josef – and you must call me Thomas . . . Are you coming in with us?"

"But what am I supposed to be *doing*?" Val insisted.

The older woman sensed, however, that by the excitement in her voice Val was determined to make sure of a share of the promised easy money. The Ballinger was aware also of the tremendous change in Grandon and knew that she would never again be able to dominate him as she had once done. And she, too, was tempted by the prospect of living in the sunshine and never having to work again. It would be agreeable to forget this dreary suburb, and to be rid of the inquisitive, talkative neighbours who even now would be wondering about her visitors and their expensive car.

"Very well, Thomas," she said. "I know what you want. Val will come with her old 'Auntie' to help her scratch a living with her greetings cards and sketches made in the markets. She will be Auntie's chauffeur and our country neighbours will say what a nice, kind girl she is . . . And how about our new friend Josef? Is he to be invisible? Is he a relation living a comfortable country life in retirement?"

For the first time Josef spoke.

"I do not say the English very well and I do not understand when you try to be funny," he said in a gutteral voice. "When we see this house tomorrow, I say, 'Yes, I stay and work there,' or, 'No, I do not like,' and we go away. We do not want other people to come and see us at this house, so maybe I am the relation by the marriage of this old woman here. I am not well and so you look after me now that my wife is dead."

Valerie suppressed a giggle while "Auntie", not surprisingly, looked annoyed.

"We'll fix everything like that tomorrow," Thomas said quickly. "All depends on whether the house is suitable. I've already explained to Josef that you, Madame Pam, design your own greetings cards and he is prepared to print these for you on a small machine which we will buy for him. Should you ever have any unwelcome or inquisitive visitors, they will be interested to see your work and even watch Josef printing it ... Now that I have met Valerie again I am convinced that she will be an irresistible sales representative for you. She will use the car we shall provide, not only for taking you to the various market places, but selling direct to shops in the district..."

Seymour's friendly tone changed. "But let there be no mistake. Remember that 'Pam Browning', with Val's help, is a cover for Josef. Without him we cannot succeed. I am the salesman of what he makes and we shall not often meet. I am responsible for getting our sort of money *out* of the country if necessary. You two will be able to use some as pocket money by occasionally passing Josef's for the purchase of something cheap and getting as much genuine change as you can. We are specializing in ten and twenty pound notes ... That is the plan, and when Josef's work is finished and I have the easy money stowed away overseas, we can remove Josef's machinery, sell the house if we can find a buyer, or burn it down. Then 'Auntie' can retire to the sunshine and, if the charming Valerie wishes, no doubt I can find her other pleasant ways of enjoying life free of financial anxiety..." he smiled meaningly at the younger woman. "Now, here are the details of the property Pam has found. As it is not far from here, I suggest you contact the agent tomorrow and that the four of us go and inspect your new home." He handed Pam a sheet of paper. "Tell the others what you have found."

"No need to read it all," said Pam. "It is an old rambling farmhouse and apparently completely isolated. There are five bedrooms, a big kitchen, more or less modernized. Electricity is connected and so is the telephone. There are outhouses and a barn, a paved yard and, most important, what they call 'extensive cellars'."

"Where is it?" Val said. "And what do you mean by 'isolated'?"

"I have never been to the district, but the particulars

say: *'in a unique position in the incomparable Shropshire Hill Country on the slopes of the Long Mynd, within driving distance of Ludlow, Bishop's Castle, and Church Stretton. Nearest big town is Shrewsbury. Ideal for walkers, riders, naturalists and archaeologists. Within easy reach of Wales and a romantic countryside rich in folk-lore and legend . . .'* That's what it says. But it sounds as if it was made for us – especially Josef."

"Thank you, Pam," Seymour said. "What's it called?"

"Peculiar name – 'Appledore'. There's a little town in Devon called that, and another down in Kent, near Rye, which you may remember, Tom. I try to forget those episodes down there. I wonder why 'Appledore'? Maybe we shall know tomorrow."

CHAPTER 2

Peter's Dream

Early one summer morning, about three months after the events described in the last chapter, Petronella Sterling woke suddenly after a particularly vivid dream. Some people dream more than others, and Peter had always been one of them. Not nightmares, but often dreams that seemed, when she woke, as real as life. Sometimes her dreams seemed to come true much later, and there were times when with certainty she had thought, "But this has happened to me before."

She sat up in bed and pushed back her golden hair. Her heart was still thumping as she relived the excitement of this particular dream, in which she was pushing her bicycle up a steep lane between thick woods. The sun was hot and a haversack was heavy on her back. Suddenly far ahead, where the road turned sharply, there came the clatter of hooves and what sounded like the cry of a child. Then, round the corner, lurched a gypsy caravan drawn by a frightened piebald horse. Standing on the driving seat and tugging with all her strength on the reins was a young girl struggling to gain control.

In her dream Peter, who knew about horses because she owned a pony, realized at once that the caravan was in danger of overturning. She pushed her bicycle in the hedge, ran forward, grabbed at the piebald's head, and, as she jumped, remembered instinctively to try to keep clear of the caravan shafts. Then her arms were wrenched and her legs swung clear of the ground. Her hands gripped the bridle and the horse reared with surprise. With all her strength Peter forced his head down, and as her feet touched the road the caravan swung to the left and hit the bank. She hung on, and her body swung back to hit the shaft as she slowed the terrified horse, soothing him with her voice until he stopped. Then the child dropped the reins and covered her face with her hands.

As Peter recalled those few dramatic moments she got out of bed and instinctively felt her body for bruises. Then she went to her open window and, with her elbows on the sill and her chin on her hands, looked out across the old, familiar farmyard to the opposite hillside. There, the solitary pine tree, which had come to mean so much in her life, marked the site of the original Lone Pine camp. Wonderful that Witchend should now be her home, and that in a few weeks she would be eighteen, and David, his parents and the twins would be in their part of this much-loved house.

Peter was wide awake now. She could smell the rich scents of summer and hear the gentle song of the brook as it wandered through the farmyard below. She never forgot that her father had once told her how this little stream eventually found its way to the sea. Born in the bogs high on the Long Mynd above them, the brook found its way down the Witchend valley, sliding over stones smoothed by centuries of the water's caress, and fed by more streams trickling down the smaller valleys which Peter had known all her life. And so, growing stronger mile by mile, the water below her fed the river Onny, which joined the Teme, which, after a much longer journey, fed the river Severn on its way to the Bristol Channel.

It was a wonderful morning to be alive and, as Peter looked across to the closed gate of the farmyard and the lane beyond, she half expected to see a gypsy caravan painted in red and yellow with a green roof and shafts. On the driving seat would be the handsome gypsy man called Reuben, with golden rings in his ears and laughter in his eyes.

But how did she know that his name was Reuben? Then Peter remembered. Her dream was not of something that was going to happen. It was true. It *had* happened some years ago. The girl's name was Fenella. Reuben was her father and her mother was called Miranda. On the day that Peter first met them and saved Fenella's life, they had pledged themselves to help her whenever they could. Fenella had once given her a Romany whistle which she had carved herself, with the promise that if true Romanies were near enough to hear its special piercing note they would come to her help. Once they had done this, although it was Peter's friend Jenny who had borrowed it. Jenny had bravely gone off alone to find help to rescue David and their friend Jon who were imprisoned in an old house near Clun. And Peter had dreamed about this adventure* before it happened.

Peter smiled to herself as she remembered this, and from the treasure drawer in her dressing-table took out the whistle on its scarlet cord and put it round her neck. She sat on the end of her bed and brushed her hair till it gleamed in the morning sunshine. Dear Romanies. It was a long time since she had met them, although someone had told her that they were still to be seen at some country markets, selling the baskets they made themselves. Perhaps this dream of her first meeting with them meant that she was soon to see them again? That would be good because Miranda in particular would like to know that Peter's eighteenth birthday was only a few weeks away. She would also be sure to ask about David. Peter remembered the gypsy woman's words to her as she said goodbye after that first dramatic meeting.

"We shall meet again. Good luck go with you. But you will have the luck, for I see it in your hand, as I see the beauty in your face. One day you will have your heart's desire, but there are many adventures to come first . . ."

Yes, Peter had had her share of good fortune. A

---

* The Secret of Grey Walls

father she respected and loved. Good health and good friends, some compensation for having no mother nor brother and sisters. Life in the countryside where she had been born, and now a job with horses which was the envy of many of the new friends she was making at the riding stables.

But none of these was "her heart's desire". Surely David Morton was that, and always had been? She remembered, as if it was yesterday, the adventure when they were both trapped in the underground workings of the old mine in the Stiperstones* and she had told him then, when they did not know whether they were ever going to see daylight again, that she had loved him from the very first day they had met on the Long Mynd. She had been a schoolgirl then and, although he had told her that there was no other girl for him, it was not possible for them to meet often because he worked in London, and the Morton family only came to Witchend at holiday times.

Three months ago, David had celebrated his eighteenth birthday. Peter had hoped that they would all come to Shropshire, but it had never been suggested, and she had been invited to the party in London. Somehow that was not what she had hoped for, although David's parents had been as kind and affectionate to her as ever. Dickie and Mary, David's twin brother and sister, had been in great form, but there had never been much time nor opportunity for her to be alone with David. She had given him a watch for which she had saved for nearly a year, and although he was thrilled, and happy that she was there, Peter was not altogether sorry to leave London, which she hated. And although he had often written – and he was not a very good letter-writer – he had hardly mentioned her own birthday.

Since Peter had gone to work in Ludlow, she had met many more young people of her own age and had begun to realize that the world was bigger than Witchend, the Long

---

* Not Scarlet but Gold

Mynd and the Stiperstones.

Her nearest friends were Alf Ingles and his wife Betty, who lived at their farm half a mile down the lane, and Peter and her father were always welcome there. On the farm lived and worked their orphaned nephew, Tom, who was one of the first Lone Piners and as true as gold, but his girlfriend was Jenny Harman who lived over at Barton Beach, and who now went to work daily at a bookshop in Shrewsbury. Jenny was a loyal friend, but they did not often meet now, and there were times when Peter was lonely not only for David, but for her old friends.

She could not discuss her uneasiness about David with her father because he wouldn't understand. He liked David, respected him and took it for granted – although he had never said as much – that the time would come when David would take Peter from him. She knew this, but in a way she still felt responsible for her father and found it difficult to discuss her future with him.

Suddenly she knew what she must do. Her dream, and Miranda's reminder of "her heart's desire", could only mean David, and there was only one person in her life who would understand her present feelings.

Trudie Sterling, her cousin by marriage, lived at a farm bigger than Ingles, about five miles away at the foot of the Stiperstones. It was called "Seven Gates" and the Lone Piners had always been welcome there. Charles Sterling, Peter's cousin, had allowed them to use the great barn as the second headquarters of the Club. And when he had married Trudie, Peter had been her only bridesmaid, and there was now great affection between them. Of course Trudie would understand and help.

Twenty minutes later, Peter was washed and dressed and sitting on the end of her father's bed while they each enjoyed a cup of tea. Having made up her mind she wasted no time.

"Dad, I'm going to ask Mrs Harrison at the stables for

a day off. I'll ring Trudie at Seven Gates and ask if I can come over. I want to talk to her – a sort of woman-to-woman chat, if you know what I mean."

Mr Sterling pushed his spectacles further up his nose.

"Yes, my dear. I do know. It is often very dull for you here with only your old father. But why are you in such a hurry? And are you being fair to Mrs Harrison?"

"I've got some holiday due, Dad. I'll speak to her before I ring Trudie. I won't let her down. I want to talk to Trudie specially about my birthday as the Mortons will be coming here . . . You do realize that it really is just about the most important birthday of all, don't you? Being eighteen, I mean. I think Trudie may have some special ideas for it."

If her father was hurt by the suggestion that the birthday did not mean so much to him, he did not show it. He was a gentle, kindly man, slow of speech and shy to show his feelings.

"Yes, Petronella, it will be good to have the Mortons at Witchend again. I am sure they will be glad to be here for your birthday. Your friend David is a splendid lad . . . And those twins! They bring the place to life . . . Yes, my dear, talk to Trudie. We must make some plans. Ask her what she thinks and then we will discuss arrangements . . . And now I must get up. Thank you for the tea, my dear."

And that was all he had to say. Peter found it difficult to believe that he was as indifferent as his comments suggested. And yet she was sure that he cared deeply for her and always had. He had taught her all she knew and loved about the countryside and wildlife, and, deep down, Peter knew that he was proud of her. But tears stung her eyes as she burned the toast, wondering if her father was jealous of David because he might take her away from him, and from Witchend, one day.

Before Mr Sterling came down for his breakfast, Peter telephoned Mrs Harrison at the stables, knowing that, like Trudie, a farmer's wife was always up early. She was a hearty but kindly boss and made no problems.

"Certainly, my dear. We shall miss you but can spare you today – we owe you some holiday. Somebody told me that you've got a special birthday soon. You deserve a break and no doubt you've many plans to make . . . Don't bother to come back until after the occasion, and if it's a day or two after the week due to you, have it on us. Many happies when it comes, my dear, and don't forget – there'll always be a job for you here."

Peter wondered who had told her about the birthday. She had never mentioned it at work. Tom and Jenny and the Ingles knew, but none of them had any contact with the stables. When she asked her father, he looked surprised and slightly embarrassed, but assured her that he had told nobody except the Ingles.

"Plenty of time, my dear," he murmured. "No need to rush the arrangements."

Again, Peter wondered why he was reluctant to discuss something which meant so much to her. She felt happier, however, after telephoning Trudie.

"Of course, darling, come as soon as you like. Charles will be at market all day so I'm on my own. It will be gorgeous to have a gossip and you must stay the night . . . Hurry, Peter. I've got a wonderful surprise for you and was going to ring you. Saddle Sally soon as you can and give that pony some exercise . . . See you."

So Peter put a few things in her haversack, kissed her father and promised to ring him the next day, whistled up Sally and rode off on a glorious summer morning. She knew and loved every yard of the route up and over the Long Mynd and down the other side of the mountain, across some marshy ground towards a track under the flank of the gaunt and mysterious Stiperstones, crowned by an outcrop of rock called the Devil's Chair. Then it was only about two miles to her cousin's farm, Seven Gates.

Sally picked her way deliberately up the narrow track

PETER'S DREAM

beside the stream which Peter had been thinking about a few hours ago. The heather was in bloom, the bracken still green and, when the pony reached the top of the valley where the bilberries were ripening, Peter recognized the hundreds of little meadow pipits, the commonest birds of these high moorlands, flitting in the sunshine. Ahead of her, stretching like a grey, silk ribbon to right and left, was the Portway, which her father had told her was one of the oldest and loneliest roads in Britain. It was still lonely because it was too early in the day for summer tourists, but as Peter crossed it, she wondered, as she always did, what sort of travellers had first used it. Sally knew the way along a narrow, stony track between the bilberries which led to the summit of the Long Mynd marked by a Trig Point. The Stiperstones were ahead and the Devil's Chair was not shrouded in clouds or mist. Peter knew that many who lived round the Stiperstones still believed that when it was impossible to see the Chair, then the Devil himself was sitting on his throne and trouble was on the way! Jenny Harman was still convinced of this and none of the other Lone Piners – not even Tom – could persuade her otherwise.

But Sally was not worried by devils on their thrones and started along the stoney track down the western slopes of the Long Mynd. They passed the ruined cottage just off the road, which reminded Peter of the adventure in which David and she were imprisoned in the old mine with a young German, whom they eventually rescued. Peter had been riding this same way and had been forced to shelter from a sudden storm in the cottage. And it was there that she had first met the young man who said his name was John Smith – and who made himself particularly attractive to a schoolgirl. Peter smiled to herself as she remembered that when, after the adventure, they were saying goodbye to John he had said, "I thank you two again and wish you luck together."

She saw Trudie sooner than she had expected. Trudie was sitting on the top bar of the first of the seven white gates

HOME TO WITCHEND

after which the old farm was named. There were times when she did not look much older than Peter and this morning was one of those occasions. Trudie was short and slim with laughing brown eyes and a tip-tilted nose. She was wearing jeans and a cheerful check shirt.

"I've only just got here, Peter. Don't think I've been waiting for you all morning," was Trudie's greeting. She took Sally's bridle as Peter dismounted and gave her a hug.

"Super, Trudie. I've been pining to talk to you. What's your surprise for me?"

"I thought I should warn you. Some old friends are waiting in the farmyard to greet you. They've been asking about you and that's why I was going to ring you at the weekend . . . Come and see them. One of them is now working for Charles and you'll see him this evening, but Miranda and Fenella are here."

Peter tried to hide her surprise but not her pleasure.

"But why are they here, Trudie? I was thinking about them this morning and haven't seen them for ages."

"Times are hard now for true Romanies," Trudie said as she took Peter's arm. "Many people are against gypsies, who are often blamed for things they haven't done. Miranda still makes baskets and sells them at the weekly markets and fairs round here, but there's always been the problem of Fenella's schooling, and lately she has been ill, although she's better now. One day, a few weeks ago, Reuben came to see Charles and asked if they could bring the caravan into the farmyard, and offered to work for him about the farm and do odd jobs. It's turned out to be a wonderful idea. Miranda helps me in the house and Fenella is getting better all the time. The other day Miranda asked about you and the others, but she seemed particularly interested in *you*. She's never forgotten that you saved Fenella's life all those years ago . . . You can have a chat with her now while I'm getting the dinner. Charles won't be home till after tea so we can have a gossip this afternoon. I'm glad you're here, love . . . Here we are. I'll take Sally while you talk to Miranda."

Just as Peter had imagined, the caravan was spick and span and gleaming in the sunshine and, as Peter closed another white gate behind her, Miranda heard their voices and stepped forward a few paces to greet them.

She was still a handsome woman. Her dark hair was bound in a coloured scarf and large golden rings were in her ears. Then she smiled a welcome and Peter, suddenly shy, stepped forward and took her outstretched hands in her own.

"Lovely to see you, Miranda. I've been hearing about you all. You look just the same, but I'm sorry about Fenella. Trudie tells me you are still making baskets – you must show me some presently."

Miranda put her hands on her shoulders. "The pretty Petronella! It's a long time since I told you that you would find your heart's desire, and that the Romany would never forget you. We never have. You must show me your hand again and ask me what you will."

Peter blushed, released her hands and put them behind her back as Fenella came out of the caravan. She was pale and had grown tall and thin, but her dark hair was pretty.

"I am glad you have come," she said softly. "I will show you the baskets we make. It is sad that more people do not buy them."

They chatted happily for a few minutes and then Miranda asked after the other Lone Piners. "We do not forget your friends, Petronella. You are *all* our friends. There is the red headed one who called Reuben on the whistle Fenella gave you. She is well?"

"Yes, Jenny is well, and happy with Tom. And I still have the whistle. See, Fenella." And Peter drew it from under her shirt.

"And your special friend?" Miranda persisted. "He was called David, but he lives far away from these parts, I remember. Is all well with him?"

Peter blushed and nodded.

"Oh yes, thank you, Miranda. If you are still here, I will bring him to see you soon. He is coming to Witchend for my birthday. Do the Romany have special birthdays when they are eighteen? We do. I should like you to meet the others again."

Miranda looked at her keenly and then took her hand so that she could see the palm. Then she smiled. "Yes, Petronella. We shall be here, I hope. We shall be happy to meet your friends again. And for you, my lovely, I see much happiness to come."

Later, after their meal, Trudie persuaded Peter to unburden herself.

"What is the trouble, love? You're not quite yourself and you've something on your mind. Are you worried about your father, or David, or both?"

"Both, really. It's difficult to explain, but I'm lonely, Trudie. And my birthday's nearly here and nobody seems to be bothering about it. I mentioned it to Dad this morning and he said to talk to you about it and then we must make some plans – but it's only three weeks away! We know the Mortons will be at Witchend, but David's hardly mentioned it. He's not very good at letters, but I can't help wondering why he doesn't discuss it with me ... You see, Trudie, this is a very special birthday for both of us, isn't it?"

Trudie smiled. "I know it's lonely for you with only your father for company. And it's not easy for him either with you out all day now that he has no other responsibilities and has retired. But what you can share is your love and respect for each other and that's more than some people can do ... He likes David, doesn't he?"

"Oh yes. He told me this morning that he's a good lad! He doesn't realize that I'm grown-up, Trudie. He doesn't understand what I feel about David and I'm beginning to think that he's jealous because David may take me away from him."

"You want to marry David, don't you, Peter?"

"Yes. Yes, Trudie, I'm sure as I can be if he feels the same. If he asks me properly."

"I realize that you don't see enough of each other, but has it occurred to you that you are not trusting him as much as you should? It may be that he is planning all sorts of surprises for your birthday. Secret surprises, I mean. It's not easy for him working in London all day. My own belief is that David has never let you down and never will. Trust him now and your dear father. I told you this morning that I had a surprise for you and I have an idea that you'll have another before you go home to Witchend tomorrow, and I'm sure it will be a happy one for you."

Trudie would say no more, although Peter pressed her, and they spent a happy, gossipy day together. Charles came home from market in the late afternoon and gave Peter a boisterous welcome. He wanted news of the other Lone Piners, teased her about all the attractive young men she met at the stables, asked about his uncle at Witchend and then said, "Hope you're going to ask us to your special birthday party, Peter. Are you going to ask that London chap, David Morton?"

Before Peter could answer, the telephone in the hall rang, and Trudie, as she went to answer it, glanced at her husband. She was back in a few moments. "Hurry, Peter. Call for you from London."

It was ten minutes before Peter returned with flaming cheeks and eyes bright. "That was David. Dad must have told him I was here. He's bringing the twins, who have just broken up, to Witchend tomorrow and they are *all* going to stay until after my birthday. David too. He says that you know all about the plans he's been making and Dad knows too, but you both promised not to tell me because he wanted it all to be his surprise ... And you two are going to let us have the big barn for our celebration ... and I can't thank you both enough for such a marvellous treat."

She kissed them both, but it was Trudie who whispered, "Did he say anything else important, Peter?"

"Yes . . . Oh yes, he did. He says he's got another surprise for me. I believe you are in a plot with him. Did you speak to him in London this morning after I rang you?"

But Trudie just smiled at her husband.

CHAPTER 3

The *Gay Dolphin*

The two Lone Piners who lived nearly three hundred miles from Shropshire, and rarely saw the others, were the cousins Penelope and Jonathan Warrender. They lived in the romantic, ancient town of Rye in Sussex on the edge of Romney Marsh, and had first met the Mortons when that family had been on holiday at the *Gay Dolphin Hotel*. At this time the hotel was run by Jon's widowed mother, and Penny's parents were abroad. Both cousins went to separate schools, but met up at the *Dolphin* during the holidays.

Later, when they both left school, Penny's parents came home to England, bought a house in Trader's Street, not far from the hotel, and took a share in the running of it. Jon went to Sussex University, and Penny, after a year at a domestic science college, was now gaining experience of hotel management at the *Dolphin* – a happy arrangement for both families.

Penny, when we first meet her on a sunny, summer morning, is nearly eighteen, six months younger than her cousin. She is an attractive girl, cheerful, affectionate, and loyal, but with a quick temper to match her red hair. Her personality is a complete contrast to that of the rather sober and slow-speaking Jonathan, who so often infuriates her, but who at times she believes she would follow to the end of the world.

Trader's Street is one of Rye's many glories. Some people call it the loveliest street in the most perfect small town in England. Over these cobbles, smugglers (called "traders" then) once hurried in the dark, hunted perhaps by the king's redcoats. In some of the houses can still be found secret hiding places for kegs of French brandy. The first adventures shared by the Warrenders and Mortons concerned a secret room and passage found in the *Dolphin*. Every yard of this perfect street was precious to Penny and part of her life. Her home, with her parents, was now Bell Cottage and her work was at the *Dolphin* at the end of the street. Here there was a low wall, always warm in the sunshine, on which she had often sat and looked towards the sea just a mile away beyond Rye Harbour. She stopped there now. The blue sky was already patterned with fleecy clouds. A gentle breeze from the south brought with it a faint savour of the sea, the saltings, sheep and the muddy banks of the river Rother as the tide slipped out.

This was home to Penny and it meant as much to her as the Shropshire Hills did to her friend Peter.

The black cat from the *Dolphin* pushed its head against her ankles and Penny stooped to acknowledge the welcome before entering the hotel. Her aunt, Mrs Warrender, was going through the post in the reception office.

"Nice morning, Penny. Should be good for business. There are some bookings in this morning which I've already entered, but please confirm while I'm in the kitchen ... And I've a message for you. Jon has just telephoned from Brighton. He's coming this evening for the weekend and says he'll be arriving at the station at nineteen-twenty – which I still call twenty minutes past seven ... He seems to think that *you* might like to meet him. Maybe your mum and dad wouldn't mind if you came up and had dinner with us here? Up in my room as we used to do. Just the three of us."

"That would be nice. Thank you for thinking of it," said Penny. "Does Jon know that you're asking me? Did he suggest it? He hasn't mentioned it to *me*."

"Don't be silly, Penny. No doubt he thought it would be courteous to let his mother know first that he wanted to come over. His room is always ready. I believe this is a sudden decision and we shall both have to wait until he comes to find out why. And you will have first chance if you meet him at the station, won't you?"

Penny had the grace to look slightly ashamed. "So I will, Auntie. It was just that I've been wondering why he hasn't phoned me at home lately. Of course I'll go to the station and thank you for asking me to dinner . . . Now make room and I'll get down to work. Who have we got coming today? Any more splendid Americans or rich Arabs?"

Mrs Warrender gave her an affectionate smile and went about her business while Penny concentrated on hers, which included being as pleasant and welcoming as she could be to the guests. She always enjoyed this and so apparently did they – Penny was that sort of girl. But she had a surprise half an hour later when a young man breezed into the hall and greeted her with typical familiarity.

"Good morning, Penny. You're looking absolutely gorgeous as usual. Have I ever told you that you're my favourite readhead . . .? I'm very pleased and excited to see you. Shall I squeeze into your cosy office and give you a kiss?"

"No, James, you will not. There isn't room. Please stay where you are and tell me why you're here? Business no doubt. Have you brought Judith with you and would you like to book a double room?"

James Wilson was a journalist working for a London paper. He was an old friend of the Lone Piners and Penny had been the first of them to meet him, when he had once stayed in the hotel.

He grinned engagingly. "No, Penny. Judith is not with me this trip. I am on business, as you suggest, and although I hoped I would see you, it is really your aunt I would like to talk to – and it is rather urgent . . . Forgive me asking, but if

Mrs Warrender is available would you mind asking if I might have a word with her? Privately."

"I will certainly see if she is available," Penny said coldly. "I am in charge here at present, so please, if anyone else comes in, strike this bell on the counter . . . But, Mr Wilson, if your business is up to your usual standard, I must remind you that I don't intend to be left out of anything. Jonathan will be here this evening, and I know he would wish me to be present when you talk to his mother. Kindly wait here," and she swept past him with her tip-tilted, lightly freckled nose slightly elevated.

James sighed and wandered over to the door and looked down on the black wooden warehouses on the Strand. Penny was right, of course. He should have been more tactful. The pretty, impulsive schoolgirl he had first met here was now an attractive young woman, but she had always had a mind of her own and a temper to match.

When Penny returned, she was at her most charming.

"Of course my aunt will be pleased to see you, James. She remembers you well and is always happy to welcome old guests of the *Dolphin*. I reminded her about your business, and she agreed that unless you want to talk to her about something *really* private, she would like me to be present. I do hope you don't really mind? We're sending one of our nice girls down to the desk. Please follow me, sir."

"Penelope, dear, I must warn Judith that I find you almost irresistible. Sorry if I offended you, but my business is urgent, because I am on to something rather big."

"I like you, James," Penny smiled over her shoulder. "But you mustn't be pompous with me."

Mrs Warrender's private sitting room had been a sort of haven to Jon and Penny through their school years. In those days, the *Dolphin* was home to them both and although they and the other Lone Piners had their own secret room (once a smuggler's hideout) at the top of the house, this pretty room, always glowing with flowers in the summer, and cheered with a wood fire in the winter, had seemed the very heart of the *Dolphin*.

Mrs Warrender greeted James courteously. "Of course I remember you, Mr Wilson. What can we do to help you? Penny tells me that what you have to say is urgent, but then, of course, everything to do with a newspaper is hectic, is it not?"

"You are *both* very kind," James said, with a sidelong glance at Penny. "I'll try not to waste your time. It would help me if you would tell me whether you have had a visit from the police during the last few days?"

"No, I have not, and if I had I might wonder what business it was of yours, Mr Wilson. Presumably you mean that a visit from the police would concern hotel business?"

He nodded and then told them why he wanted their help.

"I believe that very soon all hotels, stores and some shops such as jewellers will be officially warned to be on their guard against the passing of forged Bank of England notes, and probably French, Belgian and Dutch currency. As you know, Mrs Warrender, Folkestone, Dover and Canterbury are packed daily during the summer months with day tourists, who come over here on the Channel ferries to spend money in these towns. I know that you have some in Rye. No doubt the more discerning sometimes find their way to the *Dolphin*. Anyway, the police will tell you that the immediate danger is the British tenner, and twenty pound note. It is along the South Coast, in pubs, shops and hotels, that the forgers seem to be making progress. If they are successful down here, they will almost certainly work in London and the big cities of the Midlands. This is a real menace – and my paper has told me to cover the story. I was in Folkestone and Canterbury yesterday and obviously thought of Rye and the *Dolphin*. I was sure that, because you know me and my work, you would help me with my investigations if you can. Have you had any other enquiries about forged bank notes, Mrs

Warrender?"

"No, Mr Wilson. We certainly do have plenty of foreign guests who are always welcome. Presumably we shall have an official warning from the police and, I suppose, from the banks. We must be told what to look for. Are the police aware of your investigations? Penny and I couldn't tell you anything without their knowledge."

James laughed. "Very right and proper, Mrs Warrender. I'm sure you will have a visit any moment from a Detective Inspector Rawlings. Penny will remember him when we had that encounter with smugglers at Dungeness.* He still works in this area. I met him yesterday and assured him of my help. I also told him that I would come to see you today and he doesn't mind. We shall all be in touch with each other and we must do what we can to help him. This is a serious business."

Then the telephone rang and Penny answered it. "Ask him to wait a moment . . . Auntie, here's Mr Rawlings to see you. And he says *Mister*. I believe he's in a plot with James. Shall I bring him up?"

Mrs Warrender sighed and nodded and when Penny had gone she said to James, "Please understand, Mr Wilson, that too much publicity with regard to this unsavoury business is bad for the hotel. And I do not want my niece to become too involved or to give you special interviews of anything of that sort."

"No fear of that, Mrs Warrender. Please trust me. I have a great admiration for your son and niece, and their young friends. So has Rawlings – he told me so yesterday. He's not forgotten how sensible and courageous they were over that other affair . . . And here he is."

The Lone Piners had always agreed that no man could ever look less like a policeman. Nobody seemed to know Inspector Rawlings' first name. He was middle-aged, balding

---

* The Elusive Grasshopper

THE GAY DOLPHIN

and slightly built. His voice was slow and quiet and his most noticeable feature was a large, flowing moustache which he sometimes caressed with his fingers when he was listening to a conversation. This morning he was dressed casually, like a tourist, with a camera slung from his shoulder.

"Good of you to see me, Mrs Warrender," he said, offering his hand. "Mr Wilson reminded me yesterday that your young people helped us on another occasion and you can help us now – particularly Penny here who has just told me that she often acts as your receptionist. We are warning all the banks, the big stores and hotels in this area about these forgeries."

"But how can I, or anyone else here, know when a ten pound note is forged? They all look alike, and if a customer pays in notes I can't ask him to wait until I send for you or one of your experts?" Penny asked, reasonably enough.

Rawlings explained that the people most likely to have counterfeit notes were buying them from the forgers at a discount and that it probably paid them to buy cheap articles and get as much real change as possible.

"We will show you some forged notes," said Rawlings, "but, in fact, I don't think these crooks would be likely to stay for long in this hotel. They prefer bigger places, but they might try to pass some in your restaurant, and it's just possible that you might be suspicious of anyone with a foreign passport who stays here for a day or two while working, say, in Folkestone. If you are suspicious at the time of payment, try not to show it, but take a note of the number of the customer's car and telephone us *at once*. Our experts are quick to spot forgeries . . . I can tell you that Scotland Yard is worried, because, although a lot of bad notes exchanged here may be made in France or Belgium, the same gang of experts may establish secret workshops in Britain too . . ." He turned to go. "Someone will call tomorrow, Mrs Warrender, with forged samples, and show you what to look for. Here is a telephone number for you to call if you have the slightest suspicion. I shall soon hear about it . . . Thank you for any help you can give us. Please don't hesitate to telephone if you, or your staff have any doubts. The police do not mind being troubled, even if it is a false alarm."

He shook hands with Mrs Warrender and went downstairs with Penny. James followed in a few minutes, took her arm and walked with her out to his red sports car.

"I'm sorry about all this, Penny. Don't worry too much because I don't think you'll be involved at the *Dolphin*. I'm going on to Hastings now to see if I can pick up anything there, but when Rawlings told me yesterday that he would be calling here, I thought I'd like to come and see you both first, just to warn you. If anything suspicious comes your way, you'll let me know, won't you? *After* you've told the police, of course."

Penny wasn't feeling cheerful, but she was glad that Jon was coming this evening.

"Oh yes, James. We'll do that, but my first job is to help my aunt manage this place, and I don't really want to be a detective. It's not my thing, James, although I don't forget that with my friends we've had some exciting moments . . . Anyway, how will I know where you are if anything does happen?"

"For the next few days I'll telephone you every day. I'm grateful, Penny, but you do know what a story means to me . . . Give my love to the others and Judith would send hers if she knew I was seeing you . . . What's happened to that nice Jonathan of yours, by the way?"

Penny blushed and turned away.

"Nice of you to ask, James. He's not *mine*, and nothing has happened to him as far as I know, but I'm seeing him later. He'll be interested to know you enquired after him . . . Goodbye."

Jonathan was interested to hear what had happened, but neither his mother nor Penny mentioned Rawlings until the three of them were having dinner in Mrs Warrender's room that evening.

Penny met Jon at the station as she had done so many times before. And as she waited on the platform she looked across the rails to the red roofs and grey walls of Rye clinging to the hill crowned by the great church. She remembered that Jon had always been waiting for her on the other platform when she came home to the *Dolphin* for the holidays. Although she was so often impatient with him, although he seemed to take her for granted and treated her as a schoolgirl and sometimes called her Newpenny because of the colour of her hair, she realized that her heart was beating faster just because his train was signalled and the level-crossing gates were opening. She loved this station. The summer hollyhocks still stood like sentinels against the black fence. This old-fashioned little station was a place of happy arrivals and reluctant departures. Like life, Penny thought as the little train stopped with a sigh. Jon was the first to alight, but he didn't even look for her. He dumped a haversack on the platform, turned to lift out a pushchair and then took in his arms a toddler passed to him by a pretty young mother.

Just like Jon, Penny thought, but she stayed where she was and waited for him. He was as untidy as usual, with his fair hair all over the place. She watched him push his spectacles higher up his nose – he was short-sighted – pick up the haversack and then look round vaguely rather than expectantly. Then he saw her and raised a hand in greeting. The train seemed to leave Rye reluctantly on its way to Ashford, but Penny stayed where she was. As Jon approached, she realized how tall he was. The woman with the little girl passed her with a hesitant but understanding smile. Then he was beside her.

"Hello," he said quietly. "Hello, Penny. Nice of you to come."

Feeling ridiculously shy, she held out her hand. He dropped the haversack and suddenly his arms were round her and she was being kissed as never before. Typically, all that he said as he let her go was, "Good to be home again," and all she could say as he took her hand and they crossed the rails as the level-crossing gates closed was, in a small husky voice, "Yes, Jon. It's nice for me too."

They hardly spoke as they walked up the hill to Trader's Street. Eventually Penny said, "We've got news for you. Your mother wants us to have dinner with her in about an hour. I hope you've got some respectable clothes at the *Dolphin*. I'm going home to change. I'll tell my parents that you will come and see them later tonight or tomorrow."

Jon nodded and released her hand.

"I've got news for you, too. I'll save it for later. Don't be too long."

Penny was very thoughtful while she changed, and wasn't much concerned about James Wilson and Detective Inspector Rawlings. Her parents were, as usual, understanding when she told them that Jon was home and would come and see them tomorrow. They told her than Jon's mother had already told them on the telephone about Rawlings' warning.

It was dark, but the moon was coming up when Jon and Penny went out together after the meal. He led her up Trader's Street, round by the church to the Gun Garden on the edge of the cliff by the famous Ypres Tower which had been built as a defence against the French in the thirteenth century. They often came here. The view of the marsh and of Rye Harbour was wider than from the end of Trader's Street by the *Dolphin*. The moonlight gleamed on the river Rother as the ebbing tide drew its muddy waters out to the sea a mile or more away. On the horizon beyond the sands of Camber the lighthouse at Dungeness winked its warning to shipping in the Channel. All was quiet as Jon led her to a seat and held her close with an arm round her shoulders.

"Now tell me," she whispered. "Is it awful news? Why are you so solemn?"

"Not really solemn. Just thinking, and the news isn't

THE GAY DOLPHIN

awful but exciting. I didn't want to tell you until we were alone because it concerns this funny old Club of ours . . . Are you listening?"

She was, but her head was comfortably against his shoulder. She whispered, "Of course I am. Go on."

"David came from London to see me this afternoon. Yes, David Morton . . . No, nothing's wrong. It's exciting, but he wanted to tell us – that's you and me – about his plans for Peter's birthday. Did you know that she's eighteen in three weeks?"

"I should know, but I'd forgotten. How awful! I've got the date in my birthday book. What's so secret about it all, Jon?"

"He's got a wonderful idea. He's arranging a fantastic birthday party for her at Witchend and Seven White Gates, but he wants it to be a complete surprise to her. His idea is to get together as many relations and friends of us all and present them to her at the party. Charles and Trudie Sterling are lending us the big barn. The Morton parents will be at Witchend in a few days. *We're* invited, of course. David has already asked Mr Sterling and Charles and Trudie, and Mr and Mrs Harman know, and so do Mr and Mrs Ingles, who will put up some people who come a long way. All of them have been sworn to secrecy. We shall have a banquet in the big barn and then David is arranging a sort of 'This Is Your Life' like the TV programme and he wants us to help. People like James Wilson and Judith. My mother and your parents – and that sheep farmer bloke we met when we went to Clun for the first time. Do you remember? David has already got a lot of promises, but he wants us to think of some people too, and it's vital that it must be a complete surprise for Peter . . . We shall give her presents and drink her health at what young Dickie will call 'the fabulous feast' and David will bring on all these other friends one by one, to wish he well . . . Wonderful idea, isn't it?"

"Yes," Penny said doubtfully. "Yes. I think it is, but I

wonder if Peter will like it? She doesn't like fuss, does she? And it could all be rather overwhelming. Did David tell you anything else about Peter?"

"Not specially, except that he hasn't seen her since his birthday in London that we went to. What do you mean, Penny?"

"I meant, are they going to get engaged? It is her eighteenth birthday and I would guess that would be the present she would like most."

"I see," Jon said after a long pause. "David didn't actually say so, but I think he's going to ask her..."

CHAPTER 4

Enter the Twins

Peter's sleep at Seven Gates was dreamless and she woke happy because she would see David today, and, with luck, have him much to herself for nearly a fortnight. The twins would be sure to go about their own affairs, and so for a few minutes she lay blissfully on her back with her hands behind her head and realized how lonely she had been without him. Trudie, as usual, had been right yesterday. Perhaps David had not forgotten her ...

Through her open window came the sound of a man's tenor voice singing something with an unfamiliar lilt. Then a cock crowed, and she remembered that she hadn't told Reuben and Miranda that the Mortons were coming today.

"I'll go now," she thought. "The gypsies must be up and they won't mind an early visit."

She dressed and washed quickly. All was quiet downstairs except for the ticking of the grandfather clock in the hall, the hands of which pointed to five minutes past six. She left a note on the kitchen table for Trudie – "Gone to see Reuben and Miranda. Please call me if I can help" – and went out into the sunshine. Everything was different this morning. Yesterday's doubts had vanished with a new day. The air was fresh and clean and as Peter turned the corner of the house she saw, suspended delicately between two rails of the farmyard fence, a spider's web patterned with silver drops of dew. So perfect was this that she stopped for a moment, struggling to remember something she had learned at school. Her English mistress helping the class to enjoy *A Midsummer Night's Dream*. Surely it was one of the fairies who said,

> *"I must go seek some dewdrops here*
> *And hang a pearl in every cowslip's ear."*

Then Reuben started his song again and Peter came back to reality and smiled to herself – "What *is* happening to me so early in the morning? I'm getting sentimental."

The gypsies were happy to see her. They were sitting on the steps of the caravan, drinking tea. Reuben fetched Peter a stool and another mug, but it was Miranda who said, with her slow smile, "You have happy news for us, I am sure, Petronella. I see the happiness in your face. Is it of your family, and shall we see them soon?"

Peter confessed it was, and that David and the twins were coming to Witchend today to make arrangements for her birthday.

Presently she asked, "I know that Reuben works at Seven Gates now, but where do you sell your baskets?"

Miranda explained that if the market was near enough, she and Fenella harnessed the old grey mare and drove the caravan.

"Many like to see real Romanies in their painted carriage. We like it, too, when the weather is fine. But when it is not, and the way too far for old Dolly, your Mr Sterling allows Reuben to drive us in one of the lorries. Your cousins are kind to us. They know that Fenella has been ill. We shall never forget them – nor you, my pretty. Today we sell baskets in Bishops Castle and take the caravan."

Reuben asked about the twins and Peter reminded him that the first time she had met him he had told her that the Romany did not like Seven Gates nor the Stiperstones and the Devil's Chair.

"Now you live here," she went on, "perhaps you, and

Mr and Mrs Sterling, have helped to break the spell? I think you have for me, too. You believe this place will be lucky for me, don't you, Miranda?"

The gypsy woman took her time to answer.

"Perhaps. But for you, Witchend is *home* is it not?"

Before Peter could answer, Trudie came into the farmyard and called her to breakfast, during which Charles teased her by asking whether she would like to telephone her father and stay on here at Seven Gates until David came over to fetch her.

Peter's answer was, "Thank you, Charles, I always enjoy being here, but I ought to be with my father when our visitors arrive. I'm sure you know that we are responsible to Mr and Mrs Morton for Witchend when they are not here." This amused Charles, who kissed them both and went off to work.

"I'm not going to hurry back, Trudie," Peter said. "David said he would start early, but it's a slow journey in the summer . . . I wouldn't tell anyone but you, but I feel very excited and peculiar inside."

"That's a good sign, darling. Do as you please, but you'll feel even more peculiar if you have to wait too long at Witchend for David to arrive . . . Take your time and let him come to you.

So, after helping Trudie in the kitchen, Peter borrowed the keys of the great barn and crossed the farmyard again. The caravan had gone, and she was alone with her memories as she unlocked the padlock and pulled open the great white doors. It was many months since she had been here, and longer still since it had been used by the Lone Piners. It looked the same but smelled rather neglected. She remembered, as if it was yesterday, her first impressions of this marvellous building and how it had become the second headquarters of the Lone Pine Club.

It was vaulted and pillared like a church. The floor was of uneven bricks and on the wooden walls still hung some rusty relics of strange farming implements which Charles had asked them to keep. On each side were three big partitions, once used as stores for the harvested grain. Against the left wall was the ladder which led up to the vast granary above the barn. Peter remembered her first discovery of this wonderful dormitory and how she had promised herself that one day she would sleep right under the narrow little window at floor level above the white doors. She kept her promise, and whenever the Lone Piners used HQ2 the girls slept up here, and Peter, without moving her head from her pillow, could watch the stars swing over what Jenny called the "Whispering Wood" on the hillside below the farm.

Now Peter climbed the ladder again and realized that somebody would have to do a lot of cleaning before the party, and wondered what plans David was making and whether he would allow her to help get it ready. She wondered, too, whether the Club would ever be the same again, now that the six senior members were all about eighteen and had left school. Perhaps the twins and Harriet would carry on, but how many times more would the nine of them be able to meet here or under the old pine tree at Witchend?

Rather sadly Peter went down, locked the white doors behind her and went to find and saddle Sally.

"I promise I'm not going to hurry, Trudie. Thank you for being so sweet to me. I suppose I've been silly and I don't know what I'd do without you. I'm going to call at Ingles and see Aunt Betty and maybe Tom if he's about . . . Give my love to your wonderful husband."

"And give my love to your wonderful father and to the Mortons when they arrive. Bring them to see me soon and don't forget that you're a very lucky girl."

Sally didn't like the hot weather, so Peter allowed her to go at her own pace to Ingles before she went on to Witchend. The farmer's fields here were already tinted with harvest gold, but only Mrs Ingles was at home, and, as usual, busy in her kitchen.

"Come in, love," she greeted Peter warmly. "You're always welcome here. Been over to Seven Gates, I hear. Tom's off to Shrewsbury on his motorbike to see Jenny as it's her half-day. Alf gave him the time off as he'll be extra busy soon with the harvest. Did you want to see him about something special?"

"I just wanted to tell him that David and the twins are on their way to Witchend now, Aunt Betty, and they'll be staying until my birthday."

All the Lone Piners called Mrs Ingles "Aunt Betty". Possibly because she had no children of her own, she spoiled them all. She was particularly fond of Peter, fascinated by the twins and, fortunately for Tom, devoted to Jenny.

But Peter was at once aware that Aunt Betty already knew that the Mortons were on their way. Possibly her father had mentioned it, but, as David had only told *her* last night, the news was certainly getting round quickly. Perhaps it didn't much matter? What David said last night was all that concerned her.

"Yes, love," Mrs Ingles said as she took a jug from the fridge and poured out a glass of milk. "That will be nice for you. I reckon those twins will soon be round to see me . . . And you'll be making all sorts of plans, I've no doubt. I'll tell Alf and Tom when they come back. They'll be pleased . . . And that reminds me, love. There's something I'd like to show you. I reckon Tom won't mind you seeing this. He had it done for Jen, but he's keeping it for a special surprise for her. Don't quite know when, but you know how it is between those two . . . When I next go to Ludlow, I'm going to get a frame for it."

She took from a drawer in the dresser a sketch of Tom's head about twelve inches square, drawn with a soft pencil. There was no doubt that it was Tom and it was executed with great skill.

"This is wonderful, Aunt Betty! But who did it and where was it done?" Peter peered at the drawing. "There's a signature in the corner. Looks like 'PAM'."

"Tom says there's an artist has a small stall at some of the markets round here. Always at Bishops Castle on a Tuesday – that's today, isn't it? Tom says she hasn't been about very long. Two months maybe. She sells 'greetings cards' that she has painted herself. You know the sort, love. *'To my dear Boyfriend'* and *'Get Well Soon'* . . . That sort of thing. Sometimes, Tom says, when she has time, she will draw a head like this. Expensive, he says, but worth it. She did this in about five minutes and Tom says she's real clever because she's nearly blind with very thick specs. Apparently she's got a niece who drives a little van and puts up the stall for her. Tom had it done as a surprise for Jen. I reckon she'll like it, don't you?"

Peter agreed. Tom was surely the last person to have himself sketched, even for his Jenny, so there must be something special going on between those two. Perhaps Jenny had asked for it?

As she passed the sketch back, Mrs Ingles was suddenly conscience-stricken.

"You won't tell Tom I showed it to you, will you, love? He might be mad with me . . ." Suddenly an idea came to her. "Why don't you have your picture done for David by this woman? 'Twould be a nice surprise for him on *your* birthday."

Peter laughed, promised not to tell Tom, gave Aunt Betty a hug and rode down the lane to Witchend.

Her father, wearing what he called his working apron, proudly showed her how he had cleaned and polished the Mortons' rooms.

"Everything is shipshape now, my dear. And David telephoned me about an hour ago . . . Very thoughtful and courteous of him. Much appreciated."

"Yes, Dad. But what did he say? Did he ask for me?"

"To be sure he did. He told me not to worry about preparing a meal as they have brought provisions and will be enjoying a picnic on the way. They will not be here for at least an hour . . ." Mr Sterling paused for a moment. "I have been thinking, Petronella. Those twins. As the weather is so suitable, I have been wondering whether they would like to sleep out under your pine tree tonight?"

"That's a wonderful idea, Dad. But they would want a camp fire. I haven't had time to cut back all the bracken and heather. Until I've done that , we dare not let them light a fire. If you cut me some sandwiches, I'll take them up there and get everything ready for them . . . And thank you for thinking of it." Peter turned towards the kitchen then stopped and added quickly, "Dad, there's one important question I have to ask. You do like David, don't you? Just suppose that he asked me to marry him when he's got a proper job, would you say yes? . . . I don't think I could ever marry anybody you didn't like. Tell me now. I want to know."

For as long as Peter could remember, her father had found it almost impossible to show much emotion for her. She knew keep down that he loved her. He was proud of her. He rarely scolded except when she was untidy, and in his own peculiar way he showed his affection by doing quiet things for her.

For a long moment now he stared at her as if he couldn't believe his ears. Then, with a sob, she put her arms round him and held him close with her head against his chest. She could feel his heart beating and then his hand stroking her hair.

"Silly little Petronella," he whispered. "How many times have I told you that David is a good lad? Have no fears, my darling daughter. You will be safe with him and I shall tell him so. He is a lucky young man."

Then, to her astonishment, he put his hand under her chin, lifted her head and kissed her tenderly.

"Go up to the camp now and I will bring you

something to eat soon. I have a stock of spare rations put by . . . No more tears, my dear. And I *haven't* forgotten your birthday."

It was hard work cutting back the undergrowth and clearing the track up to the camp, but it was fun to remember the wonderful times they had all enjoyed here even before she had come to live at Witchend. Mr Sterling soon brought cold drinks in a big flask, and sandwiches which they shared. He helped her to rearrange the bricks they used for the camp fire and took back with him two sacks of cut bracken to burn later in a safe corner of the yard.

After he had gone, and Peter had done some more tidying up, she sat against the trunk of the great tree and blissfully closed her eyes. The sun was hot, no bird sang, but she was lulled by the summer hum of myriads of insects. The air was sweet with the smell of pine and soon she slept. For how long, she did not know, but suddenly she was aware of the haunting call of the Lone Piners' signal to each other – the whistle of the peewit . . . Again, and then again, louder this time.

She struggled to her feet and parted the low branches of the tree in time to see the Morton twins panting up towards her. They still looked alike, but had certainly grown since she had last seen them. Dickie's jeans were regulation pale blue and his sister's scarlet. They both looked very hot and Mary was the first to see her.

"Petah!" she called excitedly. "Why weren't you down there to meet us? We're utterly exhausted. Absolutely utterly. It's the strain of being driven by David . . . Oh, Peter, you do look nice, although you're covered with gorse and bracken and stuff . . . And here's darling Mackie. Just the same really in his true self but rather infirm else he would be the first to come up to the camp to see you . . ."

Mary stopped for breath, and so did the Scottie, Macbeth, who flopped across Peter's feet, feebly wagging his tail. Then Dickie took up the tale.

ENTER THE TWINS

"David is talking to your dad and unpacking the car and getting our bikes off the roof," he explained. "He's better at that sort of thing than we are. We'll carry on here if you want to go and see him. Funnily enough, he's excited about seeing *you*, Peter. Can't think why. You look just the same to us, but he told us he was. Honestly he did. He drove very fast. Our Dad would have been angry with him."

Dickie gave her a wicked grin. Peter remembered that Trudie had told her to wait for David to come to her, but he was here now and had driven hundreds of miles. She turned to smile at the twins and then started down the narrow track.

David was helping her father lift the bikes off the roof rack and laughing with him. He was not looking in her direction. She knew that because her father was making a fuss of helping him, he was courteous enough to show his appreciation. After what he had said to her on the telephone last night, she knew that this was the most important of all their meetings.

She stopped, put her fingers between her lips and whistled loud and clear the peewit's call. David looked up, said something to her father, dropped a suitcase and ran towards her. She stayed still and then held out her hands to him. Suddenly they were both so shy that no words came until his arms went round her and he whispered her name against her cheek.

From the Lone Pine camp above them there came a shrill cheer from the twins and a bark from Macbeth.

"Those two may be troublesome," David laughed as he took her hand and led her back to the car. "I've so much to tell you that I want them out of the way for a while. I was wondering whether we could have a reunion camp up there tonight? Can we get Tom and Jenny?"

Peter explained that they were in Shrewsbury and nobody knew when they would be back. "And don't worry about the twins, David. If they don't go off on their own this afternoon, *we* will after you've unpacked. It's too dry to light a fire up there and I know that Dad is preparing what Dickie will call a 'sumptuous banquet' for us tonight ... You're here and that's all that really matters to me, but we mustn't disappoint Dad."

They needn't have worried about the twins. Soon after Mary and Dickie had unpacked, they announced that they were so exhausted and nervous after being driven by David that they were going out on their bikes.

"We intend to visit old friends," Dickie went on. "Except for our host Mr Sterling, we do not consider that we are really welcome here. Both David and Peter look dopey—"

"Practically unconscious, acksherley," Mary added. "We shall call on Uncle Alf and Aunt Betty at Ingles. Possibly we shall proceed to Barton Beach to see Mr and Mrs Harman because we like their shop—"

"And Seven Gates, of course," Dickie added.

This was Peter's chance.

"How would you like to meet the gypsies again? They're now living in their wonderful caravan at Seven Gates and Reuben works for Charles. Fenella has been ill, but she's better now and helps Miranda to sell baskets. I told them you were coming today. You'll find them at Bishops Castle market. Give them a surprise visit."

The twins looked at each other and both nodded. "Would there be any special message you want to send them, Peter?" Mary enquired.

"No, thank you. Just my love. We'll look after Mackie for you, and if you call at Ingles tell Aunt Betty we'll be in later to see them. Miranda asked about you specially."

"Did she ask about David?" Dickie said. "He's crazy about Shropshire. Can't think why."

This question remained unanswered, and before long the twins set off on their bicycles after a touching farewell with Macbeth who without protest went into the house with Mr Sterling. The faithful Mackie was now of an age when he wanted a quiet life.

"Come up to the camp, David," Peter suggested. "Dad was helping me to get it tidy, but I don't think we dare have a fire. If you agree, we could go to Ingles presently, but if you've been driving all day maybe you'd rather walk up to the top of the hill now. There's something special I must say to you."

"Anything more than we said last night on the telephone? I've been thinking all day that we had our money's worth," David laughed. "What are you still worried about, Peter?"

"I've been feeling a bit weepy all day, David. Come up to the camp where it all began and where we all swore to be true to each other. All of us have been that. It's just that so many other things seem to be getting in the way of both of us."

She took his hand and when they were under the tree together she bravely tried to explain.

"I only want to say this once, David. I've been unhappy. I didn't understand that because I didn't hear from you for a few weeks you were planning all sorts of surprises for my birthday . . . No, please don't interrupt. I know you are, because Trudie as good as told me so, and don't you blame her for anything. After yesterday and your call to me last night and something Dad said to me just now, I know I've been in the wrong by doubting you, when all the time you've been planning things for me and keeping them secret as a surprise . . . No, David. I must say this. Let me finish. You told me last night about your idea of a party at Seven Gates. I think that's wonderful and I see now that you had to discuss this with my father and the others. I just want to tell you that I'm not going to ask another single question about my birthday. It's *you* – and I'm sure it is – who is really doing all the planning and surprises, then I'm sure I'll love it all, but if you'll let me help in any way I'll love that too. Don't please leave me out of *everything*, David, but I do promise that I won't nag you any more ... You've been away too long. I was thinking just now that what we really want is another adventure ..." She jumped up. "Now we'll walk up to what we used to call Peter's Rock where there's a better view. It's time you saw that again. Then you can tell me about all the parties you have in London and the gorgeous, sophisticated girls you meet and how much you'd prefer to be there—"

David made the right answer to this silly observation and they wandered up to the flat rock. Wherever they looked there was nothing but sky and the silent hills. They did not say much. There was no need, but on their way down to Ingles, when a glider whined overhead, Peter reminded him of the their adventure one winter holidays when Christmas tree thieves were busy in the State Forests, and again of the handsome young German she had been reminded of yesterday.

"Perhaps we'll find time to visit some of these places again, David. It would be fun. After my birthday, perhaps, or is this idea one of your surprises?"

But he would not answer this and she wondered again what he really was planning.

Both the farmer and his wife were at home when they eventually reached Ingles. Tom was not back from Shrewsbury and the twins had been and gone. Aunt Betty, after an enthusiastic welcome for David, watched them both carefully and hopefully, but as they seemed to be behaving normally, she contented herself with making tea and chattering about Tom and Jenny and how happy they were. After a while, Uncle Alf took them both out into the farmyard and said rather gruffly, "Good to see you up here again, lad. Always seems to us that this is where you belong. We've been missing you, haven't we, Peter? Good luck to you both. Always welcome – and young Tom will want to see you."

Back at Witchend, the swifts were flying low in the dusk. Mr Sterling, again in his working apron, came out to greet them. He looked at the sky, sniffing the evening air. "Rain about somewhere, I reckon. Could be thunder. Time those two were back. Meal's just about ready."

Macbeth, at his heels, suddenly barked, trotted over to the gate and sat with his head on one side. Then they heard the chiming of two bicycle bells and the twins rode recklessly into the yard, skidded to a stop and let their bikes fall. Dickie was the first to recover his breath.

"Listen, David. This is vital," he panted urgently. "Trust Mary and me to discover something. This thing is fantastic. We couldn't believe it at first, be we *know* it is. If Mackie had been with us, he would have known too..."

" 'Course he would," Mary interrupted. "He always hated her and she hated him. At first she wasn't sure about us, but we think she guessed. It's the most utterly 'strordinary thing that's ever happened to us. Listen, David and Peter. Grandpa Sterling won't understand, but you will..."

Mary paused for breath and her twin took over.

"She's the most wicked woman we've ever known. There we were, minding our own business like we always do, in Bishops Castle market. We'd been to see Miranda and Fenella and there we were, wandering round seeing if we could spend our pocket money wisely, and there she was, sitting like an ugly lump at a little stall surrounded with 'Get Well Soon' cards which she draws while you watch—"

"And we know it was her because of those great thick specs and when we saw a notice which said 'Sketches from the Life While You Wait' Dickie was VERY BRAVE as usual and said, 'Please will you do us? We can pay if you'll do us together for the price of one,' and then—"

Dickie broke in, "And then she got up and looked at us very close and said in a deep sort of rough croak, 'Where do you come from, dears?' And before we could say, 'That's no business of yours, you old witch,' she suddenly said, 'I'm not doing any more sketches this afternoon. It's too late and if you don't want to buy a card please go away.' ... So what

HOME TO WITCHEND

do you think? Here we are, just come home to Witchend and going off quietly alone so that David and Peter can be on their own, and we shan't be a bother to Grandpa Sterling, and *this* happens to us. I tell you its practically magic ... We wish one of you two would *say* something."

David took his opportunity.

"Who are you talking about, twins? You're not trying to be funny are you?"

"Funny?" Mary squealed. "You think it's *funny*? We've just seen the Ballinger! We know she's had other names, but she's till the wicked Ballinger and she's got up here."

CHAPTER 5

Appledore

Soon after the twins left Bishops Castle market, the woman known to the other stall-holders as "Old Pam", began to pack up. She never had much to say to the other stall-holders who soon discovered that for some odd reason the eccentric old thing seemed to think herself superior.

An exception was the pleasant woman at the next stall who sold home-made cakes and tried to be friendly and helpful. She realized that her neighbour was handicapped by bad sight, and this evening was finding it particularly difficult to get her cards together. For the second time the artist dropped some and went down on her knees on the cobbles to grope for them. There were not many customers in the market, so the young woman went to help her.

"Now, now, dearie. I can see you've had a tiring day . . . Up you get . . . Here are your cards. Surely your pretty niece will be here soon to pack up for you? Take it easy . . . I've enough tea in my flask for two more mugs and I'll bring one over."

"Madame Pam" found herself helped to her stool and was unexpectedly glad of it. She mumbled her thanks when the tea arrived.

"Very kind, I'm sure. Very neighbourly. I'm expecting my niece, but I am rather tired today. Working late last night on some new designs. It's my eyes. I have to draw under strong light."

The other nodded sympathetically.

"Yes, of course, dearie. I saw those two kids with you just now. Twins they were, but I was wondering if they were bothering you? Kids like that can be right cheeky. I've never seen them about these part before, have you?"

"No. They weren't any bother. I just didn't feel I could cope with them. Thanks for the tea. I'll sit here quietly until Val comes."

"Hope you haven't too long a journey," said her helper. "You got far to go? I seen you at Stretton market of a Thursday, haven't I?"

At that moment "Madame Pam" looked up and said, "Here comes my Val, and I see you've got a customer."

Not until the "cake lady", as the local children called her, had served her customer did she realize that her question had not been answered. "Madame Pam" was certainly an oddity and, although it was an original idea to draw and sell the greetings cards, she didn't seem to do much business. Next time the "cake lady" saw Reuben and Miranda she would ask them what they knew about the mysterious Pam.

Meanwhile, the niece had finished packing the boxes of unsold cards in the small van and was taking down the stall. Madame was already sitting in the front seat of the old estate car and made no response when her neighbour waved, "Cheerio, Madame. See you next week."

"Now what's the matter with you, Auntie?" Val said as soon as they were clear of the town. "Not getting tired of this game already, are you? How was business today?"

"Never mind about my business. I've had a shock and you may as well know about it, as you're concerned. Don't go back to that hell-hole yet. Pull up somewhere quiet."

Valerie nodded. "OK. I want to talk to *you*, too."

She drove down a lane in the shadow of the Long Mynd, backed into the gateway of a field and opened the driver's door. The weather had changed. Although it was not yet six o'clock, the sky was overcast and the temperature had suddenly risen. No bird sang, no breeze stirred the treetops and the only sound was the distant mutter of thunder over the Welsh hills to the west.

"Now what's fussing you?" Val said as she lit a cigarette.

"I suppose you remember that gang of kids we ran up against when we were working down in Rye . . . They got in our way three or four times. Once in London when we were on that picture business. The worst of the lot were a pair of twins. A boy and a girl with a brute of a little black dog."

Val nodded. "So what?"

"They were at Bishops Castle just now. Came to my stall and asked me to sketch them. I refused, but they recognized me, Val."

"So what again? You're not doing anything wrong and anyway I reckon you've made a mistake. They lived in London, didn't they? Or down there in Rye? How could they suddenly get up *here* and run into you? You can't see properly, and your trouble is that you won't admit that you're nearly blind. It isn't possible that they would be here or recognize you . . . You're being a stupid old woman and making a fuss about nothing."

Valerie frowned suddenly, and went on, "I tell you now that I'm fed up with all this business. We're not making enough money out of this racket. I don't like the way those two men – if you can call Jan a *man* – are treating us. They're making fools of us both and I don't trust them."

"Now it's *you* who should take it easy, Val. I've lived longer than you. It's true that Seymour has got a hold over both of us, but for the present it will pay us to go along with him. The longer we're at this place, the more we shall learn, and the more we know about Josef and the young lout he's brought with him, the bigger hold we've got over Grandon if he doesn't pay up as he's promised to do. Have some sense, Val. Play it cool . . ."

Val nodded with grudging admiration. "I suppose

you're right, but it's crazy to think that, even if those two kids were the same as those we came across down in Sussex, they would interfere with us now. They can't know that we're at Appledore and, if they did, it's natural enough that you would do some of your sketching and painting there. They're probably doing Shropshire on a coach tour. Was the dog with them?"

"No. I hope it's dead. I'll try to forget them, but I'm sure I'm right. It was the way they spoke that reminded me of more than one thing I'd like to forget."

As Val lit another cigarette, the hills reverberated with a crack of thunder and hailstones suddenly rattled on the roof of the car. She shut the door quickly.

"I don't care for this sort of country," she grumbled. "Gives me the creeps. And I don't like Appledore either. Josef scares me and so does that bloke Jan. You don't see him as much as I do. We don't know where he comes from. He can't speak English and he doesn't try to. Josef bullies him, and when I asked him the other day where Jan came from, and why he was here, he told me not to ask questions ... I tell you something. Josef understands English better than he speaks it. Jan is a sort of slave. When Josef gives him orders, he speaks in a language that sounds like nothing on earth. I heard him yesterday when he didn't know I was just outside the door. When I came in, Jan was sort of crying. Snivelling and his hands shaking, and then, when Josef saw me, he grabbed Jan by the arm and they went down to their cellar ... I know they're printing the lolly down there, but I don't like the way they behave as if we didn't exist. And if Jan won't put up with the bullying and makes a run for it, and tells what he knows about the house, it might be awkward ... See what I mean?"

Another flash of lightning and crash of thunder heralded more torrents of rain. Even had the two women been able to see through the steamed windows they would have seen nothing but running water. The ditches on each side of the lane in which they were parked were already full and the hills were blotted out.

"Why don't you say something, you old fool?" Val shouted above the din of the storm. "Can't you realize what a mess we're in at Appledore? We're being fooled, and all you worry about is a couple of kids you've seen. We've got to have another talk with Tom Seymour. We can't go on like this . . ."

"Like what, Val?" snapped the Ballinger. "Pull yourself together. I always reckoned that you'd got some guts. Your trouble now is that not enough people – particularly men – are running after you. Let's talk over things sensibly. I'm not too keen on playing shops with these cards, but I still believe that it's going to be worth our while . . . Can't you see that the more we know about these men – three of them, if you count Jan – and what they're really up to, the more important we shall be to them? They will have to look after us because we know too much."

Val realized that "Auntie" was talking more like the Miss Ballinger with whom she had first been associated. She was not such a doddering old fool as she looked.

"OK then," she nodded sulkily. "Let's work out how much we *do* know. Maybe this stinking weather is getting on my nerves. I never did like the country, even when it's fine. Seymour is to blame for everything. All very well for him to talk about living in the sunshine for ever. He's probably there *now*, lounging about in comfort . . . Come on then, let's sort it out."

The rain stopped as suddenly as it had begun. Val opened the window and let out clouds of cigarette smoke and together they tried to strengthen an uneasy alliance.

They had now been at the house called Appledore for about six weeks. It had been agreed that Josef was Pam's brother-in-law on a visit to England, who, as a skilled printer and engraver, had come to help her print her own cards. The fourth member of the team, Jan, was a political refugee whom he had befriended and was training to be a printer. Pam suggested to Val that Jan was probably wanted by the police of a central European country and consequently in Josef's power. Both women knew that before they arrived, machinery had been installed in the further of the two cellars under the house. Only Jan was allowed in there, and Pam was certain that he had special skills which were valuable to Josef. In the outer cellar was a simple printing machine used for Pam's greetings cards.

No tradesman ever called at Appledore, and Valerie acted as housekeeper, buying food and drink at the towns and markets she visited when calling at stationers and selling Pam's special greetings cards.

"We must be patient for a few weeks, Val," Pam insisted at the end of their discussion. "We both need big money. If we made a run for it now, we should not only get nothing, but I'm convinced that Seymour would hunt us down if it took him years. Neither of us want enquiries from the police, and I would not risk trying to expose them. It's possible that Josef and Jan are successful and making a lot of money now. It might be that Seymour will soon have enough to close Appledore and move on . . . He is no fool, Val. If he is doing well, we shall get our share. It will pay him better to keep us quiet. Take my advice and don't worry about Josef and Jan. Let them continue making money for us. I know how to treat Seymour. He trusts me. We've worked together before."

"OK, maybe you're right. We must give our Mr Thomas Seymour a chance to prove what he can do. As you said, he's obviously the boss . . . And clever too." Val glanced outside. "It's stopped raining, so let's get back while we can."

She started the car and whispered, almost to herself, "It all depends on our old friend Seymour, doesn't it?"

As they drove back to Appledore, Pam was reminded

of Val's reaction to Seymour when he came to the house in Stella Avenue. He had also seemed interested in her.

The evening sky was still heavily overcast. The little streams, which were a feature of so many of the Shropshire lanes and roads, were now spilling over their banks and in many places the roadways were under water. The farmhouse in which the forgers were now established was set back from the lane up a rough drive with a neglected garden on one side. At the side of the house was a paved yard in which a big red car was standing.

Valerie pulled up beside it.

"So the boss has arrived," she said. "We mustn't miss this chance, Auntie dear, but I do wonder what he's been up to with Josef."

Pam would also have liked an answer to that question, but as they opened the front door there was another shattering crash of thunder. They stood for a moment on the threshold, and as Pam stepped into the hall another door leading down to the workshops was thrown back and Jan stumbled towards them. He was a pitiful sight. Blood dripped from his face and he seemed to be sobbing with fear. When he saw the women, he held out his hands and shouted something unintelligible in his own language. Josef, obviously very angry, followed and tried unsuccessfully to quieten him. Again the thunder crashed and Jan, with a pitiful cry, dashed past the two women and rushed up the stairs.

Seymour, immaculate as usual, followed Josef into the hall. "Good evening, ladies. I am sorry I was unable to let you know I was on my way . . . Take no notice of that unfortunate lad. Josef tells me that he is an hysterical type and very unhappy in thunderstorms."

He turned calmly to Josef. "Let him be for a while. If he has gone to his room, it might be as well to see he doesn't leave it. Will you investigate? Lock him in and keep the key." He smiled unpleasantly at Pam and Val. "Poor lad. So skilful and gifted in so many respects but so highly strung. We shall

67

have to watch him carefully because Josef needs him . . . You look very well, Pamela . . . And Val as charming and pretty as usual . . . I have come to hear your reports and to give you the latest news of my activities. Perhaps we might enjoy some refreshments in the *salon*?"

Pam shrugged her massive shoulders. "Come and help me, Val," she said, and to Seymour, "Glad you've arrived. It's time we heard from you."

When the two women were in the kitchen, Val shut the door and said, "Did you see that lout's face? Josef has been bullying him. He's a fool. If he has any sense, he'll make sure Jan doesn't get out of the house before we all clear out for good. I'm going to tell Tom Seymour what I think about this."

Pam said nothing. She had not forgotten the twins. By the time they had taken refreshments into the sitting room, Josef was back and talking earnestly in German to Seymour, who made no attempt to translate for the benefit of the other two.

"Perhaps you haven't noticed that we're with you again," Val said as she passed him a glass. "We don't know how long you've been here or whether you saw Josef knocking that miserable specimen about, but while we are here, please speak English."

"Will do," Seymour replied. "I've only been here about half an hour and we were talking about printing. I'll tell you how that's going presently, but don't get too worked up about young Jan. Truth is, he's not quite all there, and, if it wasn't for Josef, he'd probably be locked up somewhere. The police where he comes from want him. Leave him to Josef, and remember that, at the moment, we can't do without him. He's safe in his room, but he can't stand thunderstorms . . . Now I want to know how you two are getting on. As new inhabitants, how are you being received? Has anybody called here? What about the tradesmen? How is the greetings cards business?"

Pam told him that nobody had called and that they might as well be living in the middle of the Sahara.

"The people I meet in the markets think I'm crazy and I'm beginning to think they're right. I haven't told anyone where I live, but if I'm pressed I suppose I could say I must have peace and quiet for my work and leave it at that. Val is acknowledged to be my helpful niece, but she can't be here all day and she's doing the housekeeping as well as selling the greetings cards to shops . . . You'd better tell us, Tom, how long we've got to stay in this hole. We think the sooner we get out, the better . . . I was recognized by two kids today—"

Val interrupted her and maintained that Pam couldn't see properly and was imagining she had seen the children before, but Seymour, who also remembered the twins, pressed for more information and it was not long before they were all quarrelling. Josef, who obviously understood more English than he sometimes pretended, was particularly angry with Pam and suggested that she had better stay at Appledore and keep the house clean and tidy!

Eventually Seymour calmed them down. He told the women that the work was going well, and that already Josef, with Jan acting under his instruction, had made a great deal of money which he had come to collect. "Some of our British notes have already been tested," he said. "You can try a few for your housekeeping, but in the south the police are suspicious. We may have to concentrate on American dollar bills, but I want you to understand that we are not interested in small money like that. We are manufacturers rather than wholesalers. I have customers who will pay us half the face value. They make a large profit on every note they pass and it is my job to find such customers. Josef, with Jan, makes the goods and the responsibility of Pam and Val is this house and its contents, and making everything as easy as they can for Josef to work quickly so that we can clear out as soon as possible."

"What about Jan?" Val demanded. "Is he as stupid as he looks? We'll be in trouble if he gets out of here."

"Leave Jan to Josef and don't interfere," was all Seymour would say.

"That's all very well," Pam grumbled. "Suppose there is trouble here? How do we find you?"

"Before I go, I will give you a London telephone number, but you must only ring that from a call box. Never from here. Use this phone only for housekeeping and your business with the cards."

Val walked over to the window. Before she could draw the curtains, the darkening sky was split with a fantastic flash of lightning. For a second, the desolate, neglected garden was lit up and she could even see the treetops swaying in the wind. Then a clap of thunder overhead shook the house and sheets of rain lashed the glass.

As Val turned back to the others, she was aware of tension in the room that had nothing to do with the storm. Pam was peering short-sightedly at Seymour, but Josef, with his glass in his hand, did not even look up. Suddenly Val realized that, although Seymour had plenty of money and power, the really strong man in the house was Josef. If his workmanship was faulty, not even Seymour's skill as a salesman would bring them the "easy money" quickly. For the first time, Val wondered whether Josef was really the boss and Seymour in his power. And what was the truth about the tortured Jan? If it was true that his particular skills were important to Josef, why was the wretched young man being bullied and persecuted? Would it not be wiser to make a friend of him rather than an enemy?

Val was no fool. She was tough, and prepared to go to almost any lengths to win a place in the sun as Seymour had promised, but suddenly she was sure that the treatment of Jan by the two older men was a mistake.

She turned to the others.

"If Jan is important to Josef, what is the sense of

torturing him by locking him up in a thunderstorm like this and bullying him? Surely, Tom, as there are only five of us supposed to be working together, it would be better to convince Jan that we are all on his side? He's not an enemy, is he? He must be going through hell up there in a locked room in a storm like this."

Pam nodded and looked at Seymour, who spoke in another language to Josef. After a short argument, he shrugged his shoulders and passed Val a door key.

"You could be right, Val," Seymour conceded. "Josef is not keen, and, of course, you have no idea how much Jan owes to him. I don't understand all this fuss about thunderstorms, but we'll give the young fool a chance. Go and fetch him and show him some womanly sympathy. He knows more English than you think, but can only speak a word or two."

Val nodded, took the key and left the room. As soon as she had gone, Seymour turned to Pam.

"It's true that we dare not lose that boy. My own feeling is that he could never make himself understood to the police if he tried to run off, but he does know the name of this place. I'll persuade Josef that it would be safer for us if we increase Jan's income and offer him a very junior partnership if he really *will* do as he's told. What do you think?"

"You won't take much notice of me whatever I say, Tom," complained the Ballinger, "but I think Val is showing more sense than most of us, and that Josef has no idea how to get the best out of that half-wit. If Jan has really got something that will get our job over quicker, let us at least pretend that we're grateful to him for what he is doing."

At that moment there was another clap of thunder, the door was thrown back and a white-faced Valerie stumbled into the room.

"You fools!" she shouted. "What did I tell you? He's

smashed his window with a chair and must have dropped down to the roof of that outhouse below. It's too dark for me to see what's happened. Come out and search for him. We dare not lose him."

CHAPTER 6

Disaster

It rained all night. Thunder rolled over the Shropshire hills and lightning flickered across the mountains of Wales. The moon was hidden by sullen clouds and, as the hours passed, the streams which had helped to fashion the valleys of the Long Mynd changed their tune. Instead of tinkling happily over their stony beds, they became rushing torrents that often burst the banks that could no longer hold them captive.

At last, as a red sun welcomed a new day, the sky cleared, and on the top of the Mynd where the streams began, bogs that fed them were under water. And, as the sun gained strength, a faint mist rose above them.

At Witchend, David and his brother shared a room, and Dickie woke first. He was puzzled by a muffled roar coming from outside, and then remembered the astonishing events of yesterday and their meeting with the wicked old woman known to them as the Ballinger. He realized that David, snoring gently a few feet away, was at present more interested in Peter than the adventures that had come their way in the past. Dickie was sure that he wouldn't be thanked if he woke his brother now to discuss the coincidence of this strange meeting. But Mary would understand why he couldn't forget the incident. Before he could go to her, however, the door opened and she came into the room, carrying Macbeth under one arm.

"I was sure you'd be awake, Dickie," she whispered as she put her dog on the end of David's bed. "It's after seven o'clock and I bet you've been thinking about the foul Ballinger. I have too. David pretends she didn't happen yesterday, but we know she did. She remembered *us* too, and somebody ought to be told about her ... Did you know that the farmyard is flooded? Maybe everything is flooded and we shan't be able to escape from Witchend. Somebody will have to build a boat, but I don't think that is a thing we're good at ... We ought to tell David about it and he could start building something before breakfast ... Trouble is, though, he's selfish. He'd only build a boat big enough for him and Peter and leave us all here to drown—"

"WILL YOU TWO BRATS SHUT UP AND GO AWAY!" David shouted, now wide awake. "You must be mad. GO AWAY AND STAY AWAY."

"Please don't make such a row," Mary continued. "It's rude to shout, and anyway you might wake Petah in her part of the house ... And don't be so brutal to Mackie. When he licks your face like that, it's to show he loves you—"

"And we can't think *why*," Dickie interrupted. "Sometimes Mary and me think the only people in the family who really care about the Club, which is, which is, disinty – something-or-other—"

"Breaking up," Mary concluded triumphantly. "Please listen to us, David, and be serious about the Ballinger. We're certain that it was her. She recognized us and she didn't want us to know her. She's a wicked woman and probably the police want her again."

David was patient with them, and did his best to explain that what Ballinger was doing now was no business of theirs. There could be nothing wrong, and perhaps much the opposite, in making a living designing and selling greetings cards and sketching people in markets.

"Even if she did recognize you, it should be obvious, even to you two, that if she's going straight she doesn't want to be reminded of the past ... And now that you have disturbed me, I may as well tell you that I want your help over Peter's party. I couldn't tell you before—"

"Why not?" Dickie demanded. "You're our brother – although sometimes nobody would think so, when you don't believe in our Club any more. You're derog – something-or-other—"

"Rude about it and don't care," Mary helped. "We know all about you and Petah, and we suppose you want everything to be a fantastic surprise on the party day. But we'll help you, David. Even if you can't tell us the most private and marvellous surprises of all now, tell us what else you've been planning . . . But don't think we're going to forget old Ballinger. That's what we mean about the Club. Once, you would have agreed that we've *got* to find out why she's messing about doing that drawing when she's nearly blind."

"And," Dickie reminded his brother, "one of the rules of this Club is that we have to trail strangers if they're sinister. You're trying tell us that Ballinger is not really a stranger to us now, but you've only got to look at her again to see that she's sinister. So what, brother?"

"I'll tell you what, twins. Go down to the kitchen and make some tea. Mary can take Peter a cup and then we'll have some together and I'll tell you what I want Peter's biggest surprise to be. She doesn't know, neither do Mum and Dad. The only other people in the secret are Trudie and Charles at Seven Gates, and the Ingles down the lane, but not Tom and Jenny yet. Peter's father, of course. You know that I went down to Brighton the other day to see Jon? He and Penny can help as much as you can, so I've told them about the surprise. Now hurry up and make the tea and I'll be with you in about ten minutes."

The twins exchanged meaning glances and then nodded.

"OK," Mary said. "I'll tell Peter not to hurry down even to see *you*, but I'll give her your love. Be quick as you can, Dickie. Come and help me and bring Mackie. It's time he had a little something for his breakfast."

David kept his word, and after making them swear that they would not tell anyone else of the plan, nor discuss it even with other Lone Piners or their own parents, he explained his big idea.

"Yes, of course we swear," Dickie said, "but what about Harriet who is coming up from London with Mum and Dad? And what about Tom and Jenny? Why can't *they* know?"

"I'm not telling them because they're rather busy with themselves, but I have told Mr and Mrs Harman and asked them if they could put up one or two people if necessary . . . Now, twins, can you suggest any other people that we've met in our adventures that we ought to invite to the party? I've already written to a few. For instance, Grandpa Sparrow has promised to come from Yorkshire, so he will also be a surprise for Harriet. And I wondered if you, Dickie, would like to ring James Wilson, your journalist friend, and ask him if he could bring his wife Judith . . ."

"And some of our wonderful detectives, like Mr Cantor?" Mary squeaked excitedly. "And what about Harriet's boyfriend, Kevin, who was with us when they burned down that old cottage on the top of the Mynd? Could we ask Harry to ask him? He'd love to come and Peter liked him . . . This is a great idea, David. Trust us and we'll think of some more today. And I suppose all the people you get will be hiding somewhere at Seven Gates and you'll call them one by one like they do on that telly programme?"

"And Peter will give them a chunk of her birthday cake and everyone will drink Peter's health and sing 'Happy Birthday'," Dickie said. "Yes. This is a good thing and we'll help you. Of course, James must come, and as he's going to help me to be a journalist I could write a report for the local paper. I'll ring him up in London soon. We'll think of lots of people. Great idea. Just the sort of thing *we* would have thought of, if you had consulted us."

DISASTER

"There is something else we'd like to know, David," Mary said quietly. "This is a big idea for a big day, but is it the only surprise you've got for Peter and for all of us who love her very much?"

For a moment David looked almost embarrassed and then laughed as Peter came in carrying her teacup.

David kissed her. "Morning, love. The twins woke early and we've been telling our secrets. Have you seen the farmyard yet? It's under water."

"One of you might have given a thought to Sally," Peter replied. "Luckily I put her in the stable last night, but I must see she's OK. I've never known such a storm in the hills . . . Here's Dad. He'll start the breakfast."

Mary went out with her. Sally whinnied with pleasure as Peter led her out into the paddock and Macbeth followed her with dignity.

During breakfast, Mr Sterling warned them that the smaller valleys should be avoided today.

"I do not think there will be any more rain. Petronella is aware of the danger of flood waters breaking loose and causing much damage. The top of the hills are like a great sponge. Our old reservoir at Hatchholt will be overflowing and although many of the lanes between here and Onnybrook will be under water for some hours, the hill itself and the valleys must be avoided. Richard and Mary must understand that. What are your plans today, David?"

"I'm not sure yet, but I'd like to see them at Seven Gates, and thought I'd take Peter over in the car presently. That will be safe. I'll ring up later and make arrangements. What about you, twins? You heard what Mr Sterling said, didn't you? Don't go messing about in any of the valleys."

"We do not care for you this morning," Dickie remarked coldly. "This is the first day of our holidays. We have our wellies and our bicycles and we have some duty calls to make—"

"Such as Ingles again," Mary interrupted. "And that

will be a pleasure and not a duty like listening to our brother sometimes when he is pompous and bossy. We shall not forget Mr Sterling's wise words, for which we thank him—"

"For his courtesy," Dickie added. "And, sir, we shall be grateful if we may leave Macbeth in your care as he is no longer able to travel as fast as we can cycle."

"OK, then, if you only go as far as Ingles," David conceded. "Don't do anything stupid."

But this happened to be a day when the twins behaved badly. It started well enough at Ingles, and although the lane was under a few inches of water, it was fun cycling down it.

The sun was hot, not even a refreshing breeze stirred the sodden leaves of the trees in the hedgerows, and the only sound was that of water running down the ditches on each side of the lane. The farm was in sight when Dickie said, "Stop at the next gate, Mary. We needn't be long with Aunt Betty, but we might see Tom and Uncle Alf. Even if David and Peter do go to Seven Gates, I don't see why *we* shouldn't go too. I like sloshing through water like this and I don't believe the whole of Shropshire is flooded."

So for a few minutes they sat on the bar of the gate, from where they should have been able to see the top of the Mynd outlined against the skyline. But now it seemed to be shrouded in a faint mist.

"It's almost like steam," Mary whispered. "I don't think I'm very keen on this morning. Do you *really* want to go to Seven Gates? I mean, it doesn't matter especially today, does it? I'm just wondering whether, after seeing Aunt Betty, it might be a good idea to cycle down the hill to Onnybrook and get a bus and go to Shrewsbury or Ludlow. I've got some money and if it's not enough Aunt Betty will lend us some . . . I don't think I like this old mountain much today. We could go and see Jenny in her bookshop in Shrewsbury."

"Yes, we might, but I'll tell you why I want to go to Seven Gates. Of course, I want to see Trudie and Charles and talk about the party and who we can think of to ask, but I

DISASTER

can't forget the Ballinger, Mary. I know that what David says might be true, but I want to see Miranda again and ask her if she knows where the wicked old woman lives. When we find that out we should go and spy on her like we used to do. I want to keep this Club alive, Mary. The way it's going now, it's only the two of us, and Harriet, who will be able to carry on. Maybe I'm silly, but I just want to show these others that we're not stupid and we're not helpless kids, but that maybe we're the only two – and Harry – who will keep the rules to be true to each other whatever happens . . . See what I mean, Mary?"

"Yes, I do, but I'm not so sure that the other six are breaking that important rule. I like David's idea for Peter's party, but, of course, he's only thinking of *her* and, as usual, I suppose Tom is only thinking of Jenny. Yes. It is about time we showed them all that we're the ones who really believe in the Club."

Dickie brightened suddenly. "When I telephone James to ask him to the party, I'm going to tell him about the Ballinger. I believe it might be a story."

So they went on to Ingles and had the sense to go to the kitchen door. Aunt Betty was cooking as usual and gave them a rapturous welcome.

"Now just you sit down at the table, m'dears, and taste my scones just coming out of the oven. Just like old times to see you two again. But what a storm! Alf was saying that he can't remember a worse one. He and Tom have been up half the night with the cattle. You've just missed Tom. He's off the Shrewsbury on his motorbike to do a job for Alf. I wouldn't be surprised if he were to see Jen again – says they've got some more important shopping to do, but won't tell me what . . . How's your David? Glad to see Peter again, I'll be bound . . . We've been wondering whether *they've* got any special shopping to do."

Then Dickie, who, in an unthinking moment had crammed a whole scone between his lips, caused a diversion

HOME TO WITCHEND

by opening his mouth wide and blowing out a cloud of steam before ejecting the remnants into his hands.

"You're disgusting, Richard," Mary remarked sternly. "Please excuse him, Aunt Betty. Nobody would think that he had a big breakfast about an hour ago." She delicately broke her scone in half, but then spoiled the polite gesture by blowing on it. Dickie was about to protest at her disloyalty when she frowned at him, and he realized that they were not supposed to discuss David and Peter's affairs.

"Ah, well," Aunt Betty went on. "We're all looking forward to the big party, and we're going to do all we can to help. We wish we'd got as much room as the Sterlings up at Seven Gates, but David says that lots who are coming won't be staying the night, and others will be at Stretton and Ludlow."

"Thank you very much for our elevenses," Mary said politely, as they got up to leave. "Please give our love to Uncle Alf and remind Thomas, when you see him, that we have arrived. There are times when he is inclined to overlook us."

"I'll remember," Aunt Betty laughed. "You're a couple of cautions to be sure. Take care on your bikes as you go. Talking of Tom," she added, "just a moment. I've something to show you, but better not tell him you've seen it."

"Yes," Dickie said when he saw Madame Pam's sketch. "That is very good. We saw this woman yesterday at Bishops Castle market. We asked her to do *us*, but she wouldn't. Said she was just going home. She was rather a peculiar woman. A bit grumpy, we thought, and couldn't see properly. Does Tom know where she lives or anything about her? We'd like to be done as a surprise for our parents. Do you know whether she's been up here in Shropshire very long?"

"I don't m'dears, but I'll ask Tom. Somebody – maybe it was Alf – told me that she does most of the markets round here. Ask at Seven Gates. The Sterlings might know."

And that is what they did. The water was draining off most of the roads as the twins cycled round the mountain and pushed their bikes up the lane to the first of the white gates after which the Sterling's big farm was named. The road entered what Jenny called the "Whispering Wood", and when the twins shut the white gate behind them it was gloomy under the trees and the only sound was the plop of dripping rainwater. When at last they reached the gate into the farmyard, they were both hot and depressed.

"We'll talk to Trudie first," Dickie suggested. "I can see the caravan and the chimney is smoking a bit, so the gypsies must be home. I wouldn't tell anybody but you, Mary, but I'm tired and fed up with my bike."

Without answering in words, his sister dropped her cycle in the middle of the farmyard and then waved feebly to Trudie as she came out of the house to meet them.

"I've been expecting you two," she laughed as Mary hugged her. "David telephoned to tell me that he's bringing Peter over this afternoon, but that you preferred to be out on your own. He said he wouldn't be surprised if you turned up here and I'm pleased to see you – although you both look rather waterlogged."

"Our brother is rather overworked and bossy," Dickie explained. "We are engaged on a private investigation and shall be glad of your advice and help because it concerns our friends Reuben and Miranda and Fenella . . . But it is great to see you, Trudie, and thank you very much for all you are doing for Peter's party. David told us about it this morning."

"Come and eat with me," Trudie said as she led the way into the kitchen. "You're both too tired to start back now. Charles is at the sheep market at Clun, so you must stay and tell me about your private investigation with the gypsies. Actually, Reuben has gone with Charles to market, but Miranda and Fenella are rather worried and unhappy. We had a policeman up here this morning."

While speaking, she had already poured them each a mug of milk.

"About the storm?" Dickie asked. "Was it awful here? But what was it to do with the gypsies? Was the caravan flooded?"

"Nothing to do with the storm, Dickie. Rather worrying in a way. Charles will be annoyed and so will Reuben. I don't think you should bother Miranda."

"Please tell us why, Trudie. We met them yesterday at Bishops Castle market and we saw a woman – a wicked woman – we have met before and she recognized us. This woman is selling greetings cards and she sketches people, but she wouldn't do *us*, and I want to ask Miranda if she knows where she lives, that's all. It's a Lone Pine thing, really, Trudie."

"I don't want Miranda bothered until she's told Reuben about what's worrying the police," replied Trudie. "And anyway, I don't think you can possible understand what is going on ... Let's enjoy some cold meat."

Mary glared her twin into silence, and he had the sense to realize that she was on his side, but this was not the moment to discover why the police had come to Seven Gates that morning.

But they got their own way eventually, as they so often did, and it was Mary who, after the meal, thanked Trudie and added, "I think we ought to say hello to Miranda. I expect she has seen us arrive. We won't mention the policeman if you'd rather we didn't, but we'd hate her to think that we were rude. When we've had another talk with David, we'll come again and help get the barn ready for the party. We're sure you don't really believe it would be wrong for us to ask Miranda about the old woman who wouldn't draw us. She's already drawn Tom Ingles. Aunt Betty showed us the picture. It's a present for Jenny. And another thing. David didn't tell us whether the gypsies are coming to the party."

Trudie laughed. "Yes, of course they are. David asked

me to ask them ages ago. They're excited and thrilled about it all and I'm sure are planning some special sort of surprise..."

She hesitated and then said, "Well, maybe it would be easier if I told you what happened this morning. The police are worried because false money – that's forged bank notes – are being circulated in this part of the country, and they are warning shopkeepers and stall-holders at markets to look carefully at ten pound and twenty pound notes for which change has to be given. Some people are often unfair to gypsies, but Miranda goes to so many markets selling her baskets that she has been asked to be on her guard and try to remember anybody who offers a lot of money for a basket. Of course, I was able to tell the policeman that we have known our gypsies for years and that they are absolutely honest and trustworthy. But I don't think you should let Miranda know that I have told you. Just forget it."

But that was something Dickie could not do. He was better at remembering. Neither he nor Mary was ever likely to forget their first encounter with the Ballinger. This was when she and a man accomplice and a girl called Valerie locked the twins in a bungalow on Winchelsea Beach in a frightful storm as the tide was rising round them.*

Miranda and Fenella were sitting on the steps of their caravan weaving baskets, and smiled a welcome.

"We didn't really expect to see you so soon after yesterday," Mary explained, "but we guessed that you wouldn't be at another market after the storm. We just wanted to say hello and how glad we are that you can come to Peter's party. David is being very fussy and bossy about it all, but we've promised to help."

Miranda put down her basket.

"That will be good. Your pretty Petronella is very dear to us. She saved Fenella's life and the Romanies do not

---

* The Gay Dolphin Adventure

forget. You are our friends too, and this birthday will be very special and important to her, and to you and your friends – and to us. We shall do what we can to please. And we must all keep our plan secret from her. Will you stay and take some Romany tea with us?"

"Not really, thank you," Dickie said. "We must get back on our bikes because the others fuss, but there is something we wanted to ask you . . . That woman in the market yesterday near you – the one doing drawings. We asked her to do us, but she was grumpy and wouldn't, and told us go away if we weren't going to buy one of her birthday cards which she'd already drawn."

"It was rather peculiar," Mary joined in. " 'Cos we're sure we'd met her before and didn't like her much, and yesterday she didn't seem to like *us*. We thought it would be a surprise for Peter's birthday if we gave her a picture of us both together –"

"Not that Peter will *ever* forget us," Dickie said modestly, "but we wondered, Miranda, if you know where this old Madame Pam lives round here, because we might arrange a sort of private interview where she could draw us without any interruptions, if you see what we mean. We should pay, of course. Do you know where she lives?"

Miranda seemed surprised.

"We have seen the woman, of course. Perhaps for more than a month she has been at the markets. She does not speak to others much but has bought baskets from us. As she comes by car driven by the girl you saw yesterday, she may be living as far away as Birmingham or Wolverhampton. We have thought that she lives somewhere in this hill country, but, if you wish, we will ask some of our friends if they know. Though perhaps it is better that you do not worry about her. People in the markets do not ask about each other."

Dickie was clever enough not to show his disappointment, but it was Mary who said, "Thank you very much, Miranda. We thought you could help us with this

DISASTER

surprise, but please don't say anything to Peter and David about it. They may come to see you this afternoon, but if you could ask some of your friends to help us find out where Madame Pam lives, it will save us going to all the markets . . . We're going back to Witchend now. Goodbye."

They went back to tell Trudie that nothing had been said about the visit of the police, thanked her, and told her that Miranda seemed to know nothing about the artist woman who had refused to sketch them.

"I'll ask Charles if he's heard any rumours about such a woman who has come to live round here," Trudie promised, "but my advice to you is to forget about her. All your friends will be up here soon and then the birthday will be over and you'll have something else to think about . . . Get back to Witchend as soon as you can. I don't believe we've finished with the storm and there may be more thunder to come. My love to Pop Sterling . . . God bless."

The twins wheeled their bikes across the farmyard, and when they had closed the white gate at the entrance to the "Whispering Wood", Fenella stepped out of the shadows.

"My mother tells me to wait for you. She says that you should go back to Witchend as soon as you can, and I wanted to tell you that I do not like that old woman who draws pictures in the markets, but if you want to know where she lives I will help you. I know people in the markets. Perhaps I find out . . . I am happy that you are here and that I see you again."

Fenella had always been the shyest girl the twins had ever known. They had never met her without one or both of her parents and often felt guilty because they did not make friends more easily with her. Now Dickie was quick to take the opportunity.

"That's fine, Fenella. Please help us. We haven't got time to tell you everything we know about this woman, but we believe she's very bad. We'll come back to Seven Gates soon, but don't tell anybody else what you know. It's to be *our*

85

secret."

Fenella nodded.

"Why does your mother want us to go back quickly?" asked Dickie. "Is she really worried about the weather?"

"I am not sure. Sometimes she knows about things before they happen. Sometimes I know what she means. Today I know that there is mist over the mountain and we cannot see the Devil's Chair. My mother has always told me that this means something very bad is going to happen. Please go quickly and take care, but come back soon . . ." And Fenella turned and ran back through the gloomy wood.

"That," said Dickie, "is most peculiar. We like Reuben and Miranda very much, but Fenella isn't like us and never has been."

"She hasn't any brothers or sisters," Mary remarked wisely. "She's lonely, but I think she will remember about the Ballinger and tell us."

Mary looked up at the sky. "The weather is rather misty and peculiar,"

she said, "but I don't think it's going to rain any more, and do you realize this is the second day we've been here and we haven't yet visited our private VS? Let's do that on our way home. There's plenty of time and we needn't go far up it – only to our sentinel tree – but the stream will be a MT by now."

Dickie knew at once that the last initials stood for "might torrent", but in his concern about the Ballinger he had forgotten that in their secret language she referred to a steep, lonely valley which they called their "Valley Sinister". This was not very far from Ingles, and they had first discovered it by chance some years ago, and sworn that they would never mention it to anyone else – not even to the other Lone Piners. Peter, who knew the Mynd better than any of them, had never mentioned it. Curiously enough, the twins had never met anybody when exploring it, and had never approached it from the top of the Mynd, but always through a dense, overgrown wood, the gate of which was marked "Strictly Private – Dogs will be shot". It was Macbeth who, disobeying orders once when chasing a rabbit, had led them through the wood to the entrance of the valley and its turbulent stream.

"That's a good idea, twin," Dickie agreed. "We won't try if the wood is flooded, but higher up there might be cataracts and waterfalls. It's good to do something on our own ... Did you notice," he added, "that Fenella was scared of the old Devil's Chair business? Like Jenny. Like Miranda. There *is* mist up there, but we don't care, do we?"

Mary shook her head but was concentrating on cycling up a slight hill, and had no breath to spare. It was now very hot, and, although there was not as much water on the roads as in the morning, the ditches were still full. When they reached the gate leading into the wood at the foot of VS, Mary thankfully dismounted.

"Although I hate the man who puts up notices like that about dogs," she remarked, "it does help explorers like us to pursue our investigations in private. I wouldn't tell anybody but you, Dickie, but my bottom is sore, so a walk will be a nice change and do me good. I don't care for my bike today."

Dickie nodded and, as the coast was clear, they squeezed through a gap in the hedge and hid their cycles in some undergrowth. They squelched through the wood without speaking until the silence was broken by an unaccustomed roar of water.

"That's the stream turned into a might torrent," Dickie suggested. "Lucky it goes the other way and not through this wood. I wonder whether we shall be able to cross it to get to our sentinel tree higher up? Let's try to get as far as that, anyway."

"Valley Sinister" was well named by the twins, for even in the long days of summer it was rather forbidding. Although the steep sides were greener than the stony, rock-strewn dingles of the Stiperstones a few miles away, it gave the same sort of impression of loneliness. And perhaps because the entrance was on private ground and it was difficult to find the steep upper reaches from the top of the Mynd, it was virtually unknown to summer visitors. The bird life was rich and varied and the twins had often seen ring ouzels flirting over the running water.

Most of the smaller valleys on each side, with their streams and rivulets which fed Dickie's mighty torrent, were thick with bracken and rich, close turf. There are many mountain sheep on the Long Mynd, and several herds of wild ponies, and the twins liked to think of VS as their own secret land. Theirs to explore and theirs to remember when they were far away at school or in their London home.

So, without speaking, they left the wood behind and stood for a few moments where a plank bridge had once crossed the stream to a wider, rocky track on the other side leading up the valley. Now the swirling water was halfway up their boots and they saw that the remains of the bridge and the body of a drowned sheep were wedged against some rocks.

"I don't like it," Mary whispered. "Shall we go on? Why did Miranda want us to go straight home?"

"*Everybody* tells us not to do things, Mary, and it was your idea for us to come back to our secret place on our first day. I'm going up to our tree if we can cross this torrent presently and I'm sure you'll come with me. I'm sorry for that poor old sheep, but there's nothing we can do to help it now ... If we say we'll do a thing, we do it, so come on."

Mary came on as he knew she would. Soon there were signs that the water was subsiding, and presently they came to a wider, smoother part of the valley where the stream had spread into a wide pool. Here they were able to wade across and clamber up to the track several feet above the torrent. Neither would admit that they were very tired. There were no thunderclouds now, but it was extremely hot in the narrow valley and the sky was hazy. No birds were to be seen, but a few rabbits, disturbed by the twins, scuttered into the bracken. Sometimes they heard the cry of sheep.

At last the twins saw ahead of them on the hillside the solitary, sentinel tree. Here they had stopped many times on their private explorations and now they clambered up to it thankfully and flopped in its shade.

On the opposite side of the stream was the opening of another valley, down which ran a smaller brook which joined their own just below them. The unusual feature of this valley was that it was almost straight, and from their lookout the twins could see almost to where its stream must have been born, up in the flat moorlands of the Mynd. About halfway up there were some broad patches of turf, and on these today were plenty of sheep. Beyond them, the little valley narrowed and they could see where the stream made its way round the side of an almost sheer bluff on the skyline.

"We've done it, Mary!" said Dickie. "I said we would and we have. It won't take so long going back and perhaps a little doze wouldn't hurt us . . . It's rather hot and peculiar, isn't it?"

"Yes, it is. I don't like it. It's like as if something is going to happen—"

Suddenly she scrambled to he feet and dragged him with her.

"Look, Dickie. *Something is happening up there!* Right at the top. Above that sort of cliff. There's a man there shouting and waving his arms. He doesn't look like a shepherd. He's running to the side . . . What's happening? *Look, Dickie!* The sheep have panicked too. They're rushing down the valley."

Then, with a thunderous roar, the high, steep bank on which the man had been standing burst open and vanished in a cloud of muddy spray. Rocks and huge clods of soil were blown into the air, and as the terrified twins cowered back under the tree, a great wave of water surged down the valley, towards the junction above which they were crouching. The sound of the torrent was mixed with the cries of the terrified sheep. They saw the white bodies of some of them rolling and bouncing towards them in the flood.

"The water can't run *up* the valley," Dickie gasped as he grabbed his sister's hand. "It can't rise as far as this . . . The hill has burst open! It's exploded, Mary. We saw it happen."

Even as he was speaking, the flood water reached the junction of the two valleys below them. The two streams were united and, for the first time, the water of the VS was, in reality, a surging torrent which roared down towards the wood in which they had left their bicycles. Mary gulped back a sob.

"We can't go back that way now. The water is still rushing out of those rocks. It's as if the Mynd has burst. Dickie! What shall we do? Nobody knows where we are. And what has happened to that man?"

Dickie had no answer. He knew that the only safe way back to Witchend was a long walk up this valley to the top of the Mynd where there would be a chance of meeting a car on the road along the top of the mountain called the Portway. Another possibility was to find their way to the gliding station and a telephone. He also wondered whether they should wait until the flood water subsided and then go to look for a drowned man. And he tried not to remember the warnings sent to them by Miranda.

Suddenly he was very frightened.

CHAPTER 7

"Call Me Tim"

For ten minutes the twins stumbled in single file without speaking, up the narrow track towards the top of their secret valley. Dickie was ahead, but when he turned he was surprised to see that Mary was not making much progress. She raised her hand, shouted something and sat down in the heather.

When he reached her, he saw to his dismay that not only were her jeans torn, and her knee bleeding, but that her face was wet with tears.

"Thank you *very* much Richard," she gulped. "I might be dead or sore wounded for all you care. I might be right down at the bottom there with those dead sheep . . . You should know that I am not the sort to scream for help, but you didn't even look round when I called . . . Don't waste your time with me, Richard, just get on with your private exploring and escaping."

Dickie had the sense not to attempt a reply, but produced a grubby handkerchief, licked one corner and wiped away the blood from a not very serious graze. As he tied the improvised bandage, he said, in what he imagined to be a professional voice, "It is my opinion that we shall save your leg, Miss Morton. It is not likely to fall off."

Then, as he felt her hand on his arm he added, "Sorry I hurried on. Truth is I don't like what's happened to us and I'm sorry if I wasn't thinking of you. Let's stay here for a bit till we're ready. We shall find somebody to help us when we're on the top."

He sat down beside her and they looked back the way they had come. Their hawthorn tree, well below them now, was still half hidden in a cloud of muddy spray, but what was left of the bluff blasted by the water explosion was hidden behind the opposite side of their own valley. They could still hear the roar of the tumbling waters, but the cries of the sheep were stilled.

Mary edged a little closer to him and felt for his hand. "Sorry, too, Dickie. Sorry I fussed. I slipped on a wet rock and then I thought you'd forgotten me. It's all been rather horrid, hasn't it? Those poor sheep and that frightened man . . . You saw him, didn't you? He looked young. Sort of wild and scary. I'm sure he was shouting, but I don't think he could see us, do you?"

The glimpse of that strange, wild figure was fading now and Dickie was doubtful. He remembered the frightening, thudding noise and how for a few seconds the sky was blotted out. And everything was brown at first. Brown rushing water and mud and rocks high against the sky. But what could a young man be doing up there alone? Perhaps he was washed away and somebody would find him right down at the edge of the wood with that first dead sheep?

Dickie struggled to remember whether they had seen the man just before the water burst out of the hillside, but he wasn't sure.

"Let's not remember him much now, Mary. I *think* he was higher than where the water burst out and we can't do anything about him now. When you keep talking about him, I can't be as sure as you are. We'll have to tell somebody when we get to the top."

Then, above the noise of the rushing water, they were conscious of a thin, whining sound above them. Mary released her hold, struggled to her feet and pointed to the sky.

"Shout, Dickie! Shout! It's a glider. He's seen us!"

Down across the hilltop a glider swooped towards them like a graceful, scarlet bird. The twins shouted and waved. From the cockpit the pilot signalled that he had seen them and pointed up the valley.

"He can't come too low," Dickie said. "He must have seen all the water. Perhaps he's seen your man – and now he's seen *us* he'll send a rescue party up to the top. You're not too wounded to walk, are you? We needn't really hurry much, but I'm not keen on what the others will say. I mean, we mustn't be too long. They'll bully us, of course, but I've got to telephone my friend James soon as I can. I mean, we're what they call eye-witnesses, Mary. Just the two of us as usual. The only real Lone Piners now. I don't think the glider pilot actually saw the hill burst out."

Mary nodded and took a few tentative steps forward. Her leg did not fall off and she turned to grin at her twin.

"Some days I like you very much, Richard Morton," she said. "Today is one of them."

There was no breeze even in the higher reaches of VS and they were very hot and tired when they reached the bog at the top. The track, which they had followed since they had seen the first dead sheep, was now under water which oozed over the tops of their wellingtons. Every step forwards was a squelching struggle. Horrid bubbles burst round their knees, and for the second time since he had felt the ground shake as the distant hillside exploded, Dickie felt frightened. Mary suddenly put her arm round his shoulders and complained that she was sinking. Dickie felt that he was in the same plight, but they managed to squelch back a few feet to firmer ground. They were still assuring each other how brave they had been when they were disturbed by the blaring of a car horn, and over a rise of the moor appeared a Land Rover. When the driver saw them, he tooted again and jumped out.

"Are you the kids Bill saw messing about in

Harkaway?" he shouted. "I'm your rescue party, but I can't get the car any closer in this muck ... Can you hear me?"

"Quite well, thank you," Dickie yelled. "We shall be glad to be rescued. My sister is sore wounded and our boots are full of water and mud and we have had a severe shock. Please come and pull us out."

Their rescuer was young and cheerful with plenty of black hair on his head and face. He was wearing an open-necked yellow shirt and blue jeans and did not seem to mind getting his feet wet and he lifted first Mary and then her twin on to firmer ground and then led them back to the Land Rover.

"You're twins," he said obviously. "That must be fun. How much did you see of what happened in Harkaway?"

"We were minding our own business down there," Dickie said. "What do you mean when you say 'Harkaway'?"

"That's the name of the valley you've been climbing up. Bill says that just before he was over it, that smaller gully blew up. He's down now and telephoning the police because he says it's full of water which will be flooding all Harkaway down to the road ... He saw you coming up this way and asked me to rescue you. What did you actually *see*?"

Mary was suspiciously near tears again, and even Dickie made no complaint when their rescuer lifted them in turn into the back of the Land Rover, pulled off their boots and poured away the mud and water.

"What were you doing there, anyway? Were you by yourselves? Where do you come from?"

"Please just rescue us," Mary gulped. "Just take us to your place over there, and we will telephone our family 'cos they don't know acksherley where we are. We live at Witchend not very far away, and I think perhaps I ought to have something better than my twin's filthy handkerchief on my knee which might be poisoned by now . . . My name is Mary Morton and this is my brother Richard. How do you do? What is your name?"

During this one-sided conversation the young man gazed at them almost spellbound. They were used to this sort of reaction, so he just grinned and said, "How do *you* do, Richard and Mary. You can just call me Tim . . . We'll soon get you cleaned up, so not to worry. I'll take you back home presently after you've told us all what really happened."

They received a warm welcome at the gliding station club house. Mary was hurried away for repairs by two nice girls, and Dickie was also cleaned up and enjoying a hot chocolate drink when the pilot of the glider came over with another friendly man.

"Where's the other one?" Bill said. "I swear there were two. I've told the police there were two."

"There *are* two," Dickie said coldly. "My sister Mary is receiving medical attention. Tim here says your name is Bill . . . Good afternoon, and thank you for seeing us. Did you see the water burst out of the hill? We did. Where were you when it happened?"

"Not right above it. You wouldn't have been able to see me because I was well behind the hill. I heard and felt the explosion. Then I saw the spray and all the muck in the air and when I was nearer I spotted you two. On you own, were you? . . . Hello. Here's your sister, all tidied up nicely by the girls. How are you now, Mary? I was asking whether you two were on your own in Harkaway. The police want to be sure and want to see you as soon as possible."

"We were alone," Mary said quietly. "I expect Dickie has told you. We know the valley you call Harkaway well, but we've never been up the one that burst – and when it did we were under the tree the other side of the stream. We were alone, but just before it blew up I *thought* I saw a man shouting and waving, though he couldn't have seen us. He was high up on a sort of ledge above the part that blew up."

Suddenly she realized that the friendly people round them were listening intently. For a long, long moment nobody spoke nor smiled.

Then Bill said, "Are you *sure*, Mary? You're not making up a story are you? Did Dickie see this man? What was he like? Young or old and what was he wearing?"

Mary covered her face with her hands.

"I *can't* be sure. I wish I could. Don't bully us. It was so quick and sudden. It was *awful*. The sun was hot and we were tired and just thinking of going back to the road and our bikes . . . . And then this man – I don't know where he came from, except that there's plenty of bracken up there. He might have been hiding. He seemed young and he waved his arms – like a scarecrow, I thought. No hat nor jacket and I showed Dickie, and then the man ran over to the side where it's steep and everything exploded and we were scared and knew we couldn't go back the way we'd come and soon after that we saw the glider . . . Now I feel a bit sick. Please don't all stare at me and ask any more questions."

"Just one more please, Mary," Bill said, "I'm going to take you both home, but this is important. Do you think the man you saw was caught in the explosion and washed away in the flood?"

Dickie stood up. "You just shut up and leave my sister alone. If we must, we'll tell the police this story all over again, but if this man was washed away by the mighty torrent you'll find him down by the wood with a dead sheep. Why don't you get in your glider again and go and find him instead of worrying us . . .? I'm not so sure now that there was a man up there, and the more you bully us, the more we'll be not so sure if you know what I mean."

"Yes, Dickie. Some of us do know what you mean," one of the girls said. "These two kids have had enough. Take them to the police station, Tim, and see that they're safely delivered to their home from there . . . And none of your funny stuff either, and by that we mean don't let your business control this situation."

The twins were puzzled by this strange remark, and when they were eventually sitting next to Tim in the driving seat of the Land Rover as it bowled away along the Portway, Mary asked him what was meant by his funny business.

"We like to know that sort of thing," she insisted. "You've been very kind to rescue us, and so have all the brave pilots and other people, but why did Maggie say that?"

Tim laughed. "No reason why you shouldn't know. I work for radio and TV round these parts. What we call a freelance. It's my job to bring in news stories and if these are used then I get paid. Gliding is my hobby, and I come up here when I can, and, of course, I'm sure that you two have got a fine story to tell because it seems as if you are the only ones who actually saw this fantastic explosion . . . You might like to see yourselves on TV – that would help me a lot. You may have to ask your parents' permission, but we'll think about that as soon as we've told the police what we know, shall we?"

Mary felt Dickie stiffen beside her.

"I suppose, Tim, that it's much more important if what you call a story like this is just for you? . . . I mean you get it first. There's a special word for it, isn't there?"

"Exclusive," Mary murmured.

"Of course. That's it. Just for you."

"That's the idea, Richard. That's the sort of story I want. You'd both like to be on the telly, wouldn't you? We shan't be long with the police and I can fix it."

But by now Dickie had remembered James Wilson, who was one of the kindest and most exciting men he had ever met. He understood schoolboys who wanted to be journalists, and was particularly wonderful to Dickie because he never spoke to him as if he was still at school. He had told him many true stories of his own adventures, and on several

HOME TO WITCHEND

occasions had shared some with the Lone Piners. He knew, too, that Dickie was determined to be a journalist one day, and that if ever he had a story which would interest other people he was to telephone him either at his home or at the *Clarion*, the paper for which he worked in London.

And what had happened to them today was surely something which James would like to know about, and he would certainly want it to be exclusive.

Mary seemed to know what her twin was thinking and helped him.

"Thank you for the idea, Tim, but I don't think we're very keen on the telly idea, 'cos it might be rather a shock to our grown-ups, if you know what we mean ... Acksherley, we are very tired, and after we have seen the police we would like to go home to Witchend as soon as we can. We've been to police stations before and they're nice, but we can't tell them any more than we've told you and I'm sure they will take us home so you needn't stay."

"That's right," Dickie added. "You'll be wanting to do your story, but it would be better if you didn't mention us *specially*. You wouldn't want to get us into trouble, would you? Not after being so kind and brave to us up in that smelly bog."

"That's all very well, kids," Tim said as he engaged a lower gear and started on the long descent to the plain, "but I can't see why you should object to telling people what happened to you and what the explosion looked like and, of course, more about that mysterious young man."

"No, thank you," Mary said firmly. "We're not *sure* about the man, are we, Dickie? Everything was too quick and scary."

Dickie who was becoming increasingly doubtful himself, was quick to take this opportunity.

"Of course you're right, Mary. I know Tim will understand. It's our parents really, but thank you all the same for offering."

"CALL ME TIM"

There wasn't much more Tim could do at this stage, but he stayed with them at the police station until a nice policewoman called Peggy had assured him that she would take them back to Witchend herself when they were ready. By now the twins were beginning to feel that enough had happened to them today. They were offered more cups of tea which they didn't want, but, although the sergeant who came in to talk to them with Peggy knew what had happened at Harkaway, he also asked them whether they had seen any person up there when it had happened.

"They told me on the phone that you thought you saw a man before the hill blew up. Did you?"

Mary's lips were quivering so Dickie answered for her.

"Can't you *see* she's not sure and neither am I. And if we did and there *was* somebody, he's either blown up by now or washed away. Why don't you all go and look?"

The sergeant said calmly, "So we will, son . . . Peggy will take you home now. Witchend, isn't it? Shall we telephone Mr Sterling for you and say you're on the way? Maybe we'll come and talk to you tomorrow."

"Sorry I was rude," Dickie said. "We would like to go back now, but if it's all the same to you we think it would be better if we went to Mrs Ingles at the farm down the lane first . . . You see, sir and Peggy, we're very fond and respectful of Mr Sterling who looks after Witchend for our parents, but he is going to be very, very angry with us, 'cos he told us not to go into any of the valleys today . . ."

The sergeant and policewoman exchanged sympathetic glances and Mary took up the tale.

"But Aunt Betty, as we call her, is very understanding about us, and she will *explain* to Mr Sterling while we have baths . . . If it's all the same to you, of course, but we are now very weary."

"Bless my soul," the sergeant said in a nice, old-fashioned way. "Take them to Ingles, Peggy, and let him telephone now. This boy will go far!"

While Dickie telephoned, the policewoman thought it wise to stay in the room, and never regretted it.

"Good afternoon. Mrs Ingles, I believe? Yes, indeed you have guessed correctly, Aunt Betty. This is your friend Richard Morton ... Yes of course I mean Dickie, and Mary is here too ... May we come and see you, please, on our way home? We are travelling in a police car with a new friend called policewoman Peggy ... Yes. Thank you for asking – we are well but rather weary, dirty and famished, and we thought that as our mum and dad have not yet arrived at Witchend it would be better if we came to you first ... Yes, Aunt Betty. Mary is here too and sends her love to our favourite 'auntie who isn't' ... Yes, I am trying so hard to tell you that we had a slight mishap with some water ... No! Aunt Betty. We have not been IN IT, but very very close to a mighty torrent that burst out. Yes – BURST OUT but not over *us* ... And you see, Auntie dear, that Pop Sterling may be very, very angry with us, and as we're not feeling strong we thought you would give us help and comfort ..."

Here he paused and held the receiver away from his ear as Mrs Ingles expressed sorrow, curiosity, welcome and an abiding affection for her darlings at the top of her voice. When she stopped to take breath, Mary took the telephone.

"Lovely to hear your voice, dear Aunt Betty. We're on our way and there is just one little thing. We think it would be best if you keep all this a secret until we come, and then we can explain. It wouldn't be fair to worry Pop, would it? He gets anxious about us sometimes, and there's no need to tell David or Peter, 'cos we expect they're busy somewhere minding their own business ... Yes, dear Auntie, we are rather muddy and tired, but people have been so kind to us ... See you soon."

"I'm looking forward to meeting your Mrs Ingles," Peggy said briskly as she replaced the telephone. "Do you both often give that sort of performance?"

"Not often," Dickie admitted. "Sometimes, though, we want somebody to do something without having time to ask us too many questions. And Aunt Betty does talk a very, very long time on the telephone and Uncle Alf – that's her husband – told her once when we were there, that her talks on the telephone would ruin him and he'd have to sell the farm and we wouldn't like that at all . . . But we should like you to meet her because she is very nice."

Twenty minutes later, Peggy stopped the car outside the farmyard gate of Ingles.

"Just before you go in," she said, "I want to ask you again whether anything you saw or heard today has not been told to the people at the gliding club or to me. We know you've done nothing wrong, although it seems to me that if you'd had more sense you wouldn't have gone up Harkaway by yourselves after you'd been told not to. I know you don't feel sure about seeing a man up there before the explosion and I'm not surprised at that, so don't worry about it. If later on, perhaps tomorrow, you can remember better, just let us know. I think you both have been very brave and sensible and I'm sure our sergeant does too – but please, twins, if you do remember more about that man, tell us at once. We know each other now, and I hope you'll feel I'm one of your friends . . . You see, it is just possible that the man was somebody the police want to help – or indeed somebody who can help them as much as you can by remembering more. See what I mean?"

"Yes, we do," Dickie admitted, although he was still thinking that the man he wanted most to help was James Wilson, so that it was Mary who added, "But, Peggy, we do like helping the police very much. We've often done it and acksherley we're quite good at it. One of your great detectives up here in Shropshire is a friend of ours. We've helped him a lot, haven't we, Dickie?"

"You mean Mr Cantor. Everybody calls him Mister,

don't they? Do you know him, Peggy? We thought you might. He knows all about us, doesn't he, Mary?"

"Of course. Please give him our love and say he will be very welcome at Witchend any time and so will you. Now here's Aunt Betty at the gate. Come and meet her and thank you for taking such care of us."

It took ten minutes to escape from Aunt Betty's welcome and to say goodbye to the twins, but before starting the car WPC Peggy used her radio telephone and asked to speak to Detective Inspector Cantor.

CHAPTER 8

David and Peter Go Shopping

Not long after the twins had set off on their expedition which so nearly ended in disaster, David drove Peter into Shrewsbury. They were alone with Mr Sterling for ten minutes before they left and he walked with them over to the car, then unexpectedly kissed his daughter and solemnly shook hands with David.

Peter turned to wave as David turned into the lane, and after a short silence while she dabbed her eyes, he said, "Anyone would think that he won't see us for weeks. Acksherley, as Mary would say, I like and admire your dad very much. And not just because of you, either. It's good to know that he approves of us . . . Cheer up, love. You're not going to a funeral . . . Did you telephone Jenny to say that we're going to take her out to lunch? Not a word to her about the object of our exercise. We've just been choosing your birthday present. Have you seen much of Jen lately?" he added. "Or Tom?"

"Not much. Tom's busy all the time at Ingles this time of year, and it's awful to think what's happening to the harvest after the storm, but on his days off he goes over to Shrewsbury to see Jenny. She loves her job. I think she took it because when there aren't customers in the shop she can read some sloppy novel! She's fun, David, but as my job at the stables is so different we don't see much of each other now. That's why us all meeting together again is so important. I'm not sure what's going on between her and

Tom. Maybe *they've* got a secret too . . ." She glanced at him. "I'm glad you like my dad. He can't often say what he feels straight out, but he was so sweet just now that he made me cry. Thank you for being so nice to him."

"Lucky old me," David said quietly and, for a moment, clasped her hand on her lap. "Let's do our shopping first. You've made up your mind about what you want, haven't you?"

The rest of the journey was uneventful, although there was plenty of water on the main road. David knew where he wanted to park in Shrewsbury and what he called "the birthday shop" was not far from Dawkins Book Store where Jenny worked.

They were nearly half an hour in the first shop and when they came out, hand in hand, Peter was flushed and looking very pretty.

"You really do like it, darling?" he said. "Pity it didn't quite fit – but we've got time."

She nodded. "Everything is so wonderful I can hardly believe it's true. If I didn't know you better, some people might think that you'd done it before! Let's go and see Jen – but not a word about my birthday present."

"I suppose we must collect her, but I wish now that we hadn't asked her out today. Just the two of us would have been more appropriate. Sorry, Peter."

"Nonsense. Of course we're going to take her out. I'm looking forward to Jen. I always do, but we shall look a bit silly if Tom has turned up."

There were no customers in the shop when they went in, and Jenny was alone behind the counter. She was a few months older than Peter, but slighter and slimmer. A redhead with an eager, freckled face, impulsive and warmhearted, but never vain. This morning, as she welcomed them, she was so excited that she looked exceptionally pretty.

She leaned across the piles of papers on the counter, grabbed David and kissed him.

DAVID AND PETER GO SHOPPING

"And you, Peter! It's wonderful to see you both. You look absolutely fantastic, Peter, and thank you for asking me out. I love being taken out. Tom does when he can, but I haven't seen David for years and years, and I don't often see Peter to ask her about you, and now I've got you both . . . And before I tell the most exciting and utterly fantastic news which has happened to us here this morning, just tell me about the others. The twins I mean. Are they here yet? And Harriet? And Penny and Jon? I know they're all coming to the party. You must tell me more about that, David. I'm out of touch. Nobody tells me *anything*. Except Tom, of course, but he doesn't talk much really—"

Here Jenny paused for breath and David said hurriedly, "He doesn't have much chance when he's with you, does he, Jen? We'll give you our news presently, but what's happened to you this morning? What's the utterly fantastic news that's happened in this shop?"

Jenny squeezed herself round the end of the counter, unexpectedly opened the shop door, looked each way into the street, came back and stood between her friends.

"Listen," she whispered, "I don't suppose that what has happened is a real secret, but this morning, 'bout an hour ago, we had a visit from an absolutely wonderful policeman. Yes, honestly! I don't think that what he told us was a secret, but it was very, very vital. There's a big crime going on round here, and the police want us to help, so I'm sure this superman wouldn't mind you knowing because it will soon be in the news . . . Oh! Here's Mr Dawkins! They're from Witchend near where I live. I've known them for years. They're friends of Tom too and I was just about to tell them about our policeman, but maybe it would be better if you did."

Mr Dawkins was tall and thin with a bushy moustache and a bald head. He was a nice man but usually rather depressed. Although he obviously liked Jenny, and admired her enthusiasm for books and her pleasant ways with

105

HOME TO WITCHEND

customers, there must have been times when he wondered whether he would ever be able to express his own opinions and wishes. Now he smiled at David and Peter, liked what he saw and said:

"Good morning. I've always wanted to meet friends of Jenny. As she is apparently telling you of our visitor this morning, there seems no reason why you should not hear what has happened. If I don't tell you, she most certainly will, and I understand the police will shortly be asking for the help of us all." Mr Dawkins cleared his throat. "Shopkeepers in the West Midlands are being warned that in this area in particular there are a number of forged ten and twenty pound notes in circulation. I have had no experience of this sort of trouble, but it seems that the forgers – or those who buy from them – choose shops where the goods on sale are comparatively cheap, offer a ten pound note for something costing, say, fifty pence, like one of these greetings cards, and get nine pounds fifty in change in genuine money. I was asked this morning to take particular notice of anyone offering a ten or twenty pound note. I have told Jenny that we must ask for the exact money for the item and say we have not the change available and, if we can, to remember the number of the note offered. If the customer comes by car, we should try to take its number. Banks, of course, know what to look for, but as I told the copper this morning, I can't chat to every customer who offers a tenner or twenty while Jenny runs to the bank with it. Anyway, I reckon there'll be such a rumpus about this racket that we shan't have much to worry about ... You wouldn't think these crooks would have such a nerve, would you?"

"Is there any way ordinary people can recognize a bad note?" David asked. "How would *I* know?"

The depressed Mr Dawkins shrugged. "I'm not sure. Business is difficult enough anyway. I don't know what this country is coming to. I suppose the banks will warn us what to look for. I bet they're busy looking through their stock right now . . ." He stroked his moustache gloomily. "If you three want to get off now, Jenny can go," he said. "Back in an hour."

Jenny filled sixty minutes with her chatter.

"Now don't you worry where to take me, David, I can tell you a fantastic place. It's quite near and where Tom takes me when he can. Not too big. It's called *The Magic Lantern* and it's cosy and rather romantic. Nearly all the people who come know each other, and I was saying to Tom only the other day, that it's just the sort of place David ought to bring Peter and that's why I want to show it to you . . . Maybe, if you're going to stay long at Witchend, you'll bring her sometimes. I want to talk to you about that – but here we are and I hope you like it – " And she took a deep breath as David opened the door of a small café and followed her in. Jenny may have thought the atmosphere of the Lantern was romantic but he thought it gloomy and rather stuffy. As Jenny stepped forward to speak to a waitress in what was supposed to be a Japanese costume, Peter took his hand and whispered, "Don't spoil it for her, David. She's having a gorgeous time." Then Jenny introduced the waitress. "These are my special friends, Anne. Not as special as Tom, of course, but nearly. And please my we have the table in the corner?"

Anne, with a welcoming Shropshire smile, led them into the gloom and then, as soon as they had finished their soup, Jenny was off again.

"There's something very important and private I want to ask you, David. Tom and me were talking about it, and think you ought to know that you should come up here more often. To Witchend, I mean. I suppose you know that Peter pines for you? Of course, I pine for Tom when I don't see him, but Peter's is a worse pine because she hardly ever *does* see you . . . You mustn't be angry with me, but we think you're deserting Peter."

"Not for long, Jenny. Not really and not always, but

thank you and Tom for thinking of us."

"That's all right, David. It's just that next to Tom, who is different, I love Peter and you best in all the world."

For a few moments there was silence. Peter felt for David's hand under the table and when they looked at Jenny in astonishment they saw tears on her cheeks.

"Thank you, Jen," Peter said quickly. "We love you too. I'll never forget the day we met on the way to Seven Gates, and the way you've helped to make the Lone Piners mean something to us all. And now let's stop being solemn. What have you and Tom been up to?"

Jenny gave them her radiant smile.

"I was going to ask *you* that. Have you been shopping this morning?"

"You've guessed it," David agreed. "We've been choosing Peter's birthday present."

"How wonderful!" Jenny sighed. "I bet it's a ring. It ought to be a ring. All of us Lone Piners, specially Tom, think it ought to be a ring."

"And what about Tom?" David asked. "I haven't seen him yet. What does he think about rings? He's a man with a responsible job and you're working now. When I see your dad at Peter's party next week, I shall ask him what he thinks about your prospects."

"OK," Jenny laughed. "You ask him. He likes you. I was going to ask about the party. What can we do to help?"

"Lots, Jenny. Get Tom to bring you down to Ingles soon and I'll come round and talk it over with you. With your help I've got a special surprise for Peter – she knows it's a secret. Jon and Penny are coming from Rye in a day or two, so I may be able to bring them. Aunt Betty is helping and your mum and dad will if they can. But Peter doesn't know and you're not to tell her when you know. We're going to be busy, Jen."

"That's OK. We'll help – and don't try to arrange too much without us." Jenny stood up. "Cheerio both. I must get back now. I'm a businesswoman. Thank you, David, for a lovely party."

She blew kisses to them both and the *Magic Lantern* was a little gloomier when she had gone.

"I suppose Tom never tries to answer her back," David wondered. "He hasn't a chance, has he?"

"I don't think he wants one, David! We'll be lucky in the future if we ever have a truer friend than Jenny. What shall we do now? Maybe we should go home and tell Dad what we've been up to, and see if the twins are back. I don't think it's rained again, but they've probably been messing about with water somewhere."

"Maybe we should do that, love, but I don't think we need worry. Before we go back, I'd like to look in at the market. Maybe I could find a little something I could buy you as a special souvenir of today."

"Or something we could buy for each other? That would be better still. But there's something else on your mind, isn't there? That woman the twins saw at the Castle market? The woman who wouldn't draw them and that you've had trouble with down at Rye? The Ballinger? I've never seen her, but after their description of her I think I should recognize her."

"Yes, Peter. That's the woman. You know that the twins aren't stupid about this sort of thing, and it's true that she really was a very wicked woman. Pity Jon and Penny aren't here, because they were the first of us all to meet her. But even if this woman is the Ballinger, we needn't get involved. I admit I'm curious though, and she really *was* an artist when we first knew about her. If she's any good, I'd like her to sketch you. She wouldn't recognise *me*. D'you mind? We can wander round the shops first."

They spent a happy hour window-shopping. Neither of them were great talkers, and they were now so happy together that there seemed no need for words, but eventually Peter said, "If you really want to see that woman, we'd better go to the market now. I don't want Dad to be alone too long – especially as he was so sweet to us this morning. He'll want our news, darling."

Madame Pam was behind her stall in the market, and as she was serving an old lady with a greetings card, David was able to watch her closely. The woman he had last known to be the Ballinger had called herself Madame Christabel and, among other activities, had run a smart dress shop in London.* She was much slimmer and smarter than this woman, who was untidy and wearing a check tweed jacket over a shabby dress. Madame Christabel had blue-rinsed hair, this woman's was grey under a shapeless felt hat. But David remembered that their friends the Warrenders, who had seen more of her down in Sussex, had once told him that the Ballinger's voice was unforgettably loud and harsh, and that she always wore spectacles with particularly strong lenses. Madame Pam was certainly wearing those.

Suddenly David was sure that the twins were right. The fact that they should meet again in Shropshire at first seemed incredible, but coincidences usually were surprising. As the customer paid for her card, David took Peter's hand and led her forward. He made no attempt to disguise himself, because, even if this was the Ballinger who had recognized the twins, she would be unlikely to remember him. As friends had often remarked with some feeling, the twins were unforgettable. So quite normally David said, "Good afternoon. If you are not too busy, we'd like a sketch of my friend here."

The woman peered at them short-sightedly, took off her spectacles and leaned across the counter to study Peter's face more closely. Then she replaced her specs and said in a hoarse, deep voice,

"Sit down on the stool, please, girl, and don't look at me. Payment in advance."

* Lone Pine London

DAVID AND PETER GO SHOPPING

Peter tried not to look as annoyed as she felt. Whether or not David and the twins had met this rude woman before, she already disliked her. But she sat down obediently and tried not to feel, or look, embarrassed, as three children gathered round as an audience.

After an encouraging wink and a smile, David passed over the money and, hoping to save Peter further embarrassment, strolled over to the next stall. Here a cheerful man was selling all sorts of electrical equipment, including pocket calculators and radio sets, one of which was announcing its charms with pop music. David was mildly interested and wondered whether a small set like this would be appreciated by Mr Sterling, whose only radio at Witchend was a very old set which was quite unsuitable for anything much except the News – which often seemed to depress him as much as pop music. David wanted very much to give Peter's father a present and decided to ask Peter's advice. He looked across to see how she was getting on, waved to her and, at that moment, the music stopped suddenly and the disc jockey announced a news flash:

"News has just come through from one of our special reporters of particular interest to listeners in the Shropshire hill country. This morning, a dramatic and dangerous water explosion occurred in a lonely valley known as Harkaway Hollow in the Long Mynd. Tons of released water, pent up in the bogs after the recent thunderstorms at the head of the many valleys on the eastern escarpment of the mountain, have burst out of the hillside and for some hours the deluge has been roaring down the valley, devastating everything in its path. Hundreds of sheep have been drowned. News of this catastrophe has been brought by a glider pilot from the Midland Gliding Club on the top of the Mynd, who was a chance witness of the explosion. Other witnesses appear to be two children who were exploring the Hollow, but were fortunately higher up the valley when the explosion occurred below them. Our reporter, Tim Carter, happened to be in the clubhouse and rescued the two children in his Land Rover just as they reached the top of the Harkaway. They are exhausted, but otherwise unhurt, and were taken to the police to make their report and are now safe at Witchend Farmhouse where they are staying. Obviously, after such an alarming experience, their report of the actual calamity is a little uncertain. One of them believes that a few seconds before the actual explosion she saw a man on the hillside waving his arms. They cannot agree that they saw him engulfed or carried away by the flood waters, but the police have been informed, and we hear that some local farmers are on their way now to search the mountain and Harkaway where the flood is now subsiding. More news in the next bulletin."

The proprietor switched off and turned to David, "Anything here you fancy, son? All bargains. Everything guaranteed. Lucky escape for those kids up the Mynd, I reckon. There was a water burst like that some years ago."

David, feeling slightly sick and very angry, shook his head and hurried back to Peter, who was standing up with her sketch in her hand.

"It's not bad, David – I like it . . . What *is* the matter? What's happened?"

He grabbed her arm, but before he could give her the news, a young woman pushed rudely past them and they distinctly heard what she said to Madame Pam.

"Pack up at once. We must get back. The two men are fussing. There's been a flood in one of the valleys and some kids say they saw a man washed away. Could be *him*. Hurry!"

CHAPTER 9

Enter Mr Cantor

Peter had no chance to show the sketch to David who quickly led her out of earshot.

"Sorry, Pete. We're in a hurry. I've just heard a news flash on the radio. The twins are in trouble again, and I'm so angry you'll have to hold me back when we do see them. In spite of what we all told them, they've been in a valley I've never heard of – Harkaway or some such name – where there's been a water explosion, and the kids say they saw a man waving his arms and he disappeared. Apparently they got to the top of the main valley and were rescued by a bloke from the gliding club and are now with the police . . . They can't be trusted out of our sight, Pete, and I'm fed up with them. Can you *imagine* what my parents will say?"

"Keep your cool, David," Peter said as he hustled her through the crowded market to the car. "The important thing is that they're safe, but I shudder to think what my dad will say. Luckily he doesn't listen to the radio at this time of day, and never to the news if he can avoid it. But surely he made the twins promise not to go into any of the valleys this morning?"

"Yes, he did. Why did they choose Harkaway, I wonder. Do you know it? Is it particularly dangerous?"

"Shouldn't have thought so. I believe I've been up it once on Sally. Not many people know about it, and it's certainly off the tourist routes . . . Come to think of it, David,

I believe there was a water explosion there a few years ago . . . And you needn't grab my arm quite so hard: I'm coming as fast as I can. Why the hurry?"

"I'm not worried about the twins, love. I'm worried about your dad and what he will think when they're brought to Witchend in a police car. The announcer mentioned Witchend and it's possible some listeners have already rung up. I don't want to spoil this fantastic day, darling, but the twins are my responsibility and I'm not going to have your father upset by any message that may have come through . . . I wanted this to be our day – specially yours – and now look what's happened."

"Yes. I see what you mean about Dad. Maybe we could give him my sketch and calm him down? You give it to him as a souvenir of today – and I haven't even thanked you for it yet."

David didn't say much at first as he drove back to Witchend. He did not want to spoil Peter's day by delving into the past, but the more he thought about it, the more certain he became that the twins were right, and that Madame Pam, the artist working the markets, was the Ballinger they first saw in Rye some years ago at the same time as they met Jon and Penny Warrender. She looked older now, of course, and not much like the smart Madame Christabel in London. But the voice was the same and so were the exceptionally thick specs. And then, with a sudden sense of shock, David remembered that in the London adventure she was involved in a racket of forging pictures, and that the expensive dress shop she ran was only a blind. And there was a young woman accomplice whose name he could not remember, but it could be the same girl who had just warned the Ballinger and hurried her away with an allusion to a missing man.

And now, in this unlikely country, there was new evidence of forgery, and it was more than likely that the half-blind old woman who, in a few minutes had caught in a

ENTER MR CANTOR

rough sketch Peter's beauty, was again involved in the same sort of crime.

"David! Look where you're going!" Peter called urgently. "Pull up in that lay-by and tell me what's on your mind. You're not concentrating."

He obeyed, put his arm round her, apologized and told her everything.

"You weren't with us in Brownlow Square then, but we did tell you all about it. Of course you remember Dickie's journalist hero James Wilson. He was on that forgery story and a great help to us, and I wonder whether he's on this story too? It's amazing that this should be happening to us, up here, at this time. I wanted it to be all yours. Every minute of it from this morning until your birthday. Before we know where we are, we'll have Mister Cantor calling at Witchend. Bloke on the news flash said that a few local farmers were searching for the man Mary *thinks* she saw, and probably Tom and Uncle Alf will be on that. How much of all this Ballinger business are we going to tell your father?"

"Nothing yet, please, With the twins, we're the only four who know, but we must warn those two. Drive straight to Witchend now and find out whether Dad has heard about the water explosion . . . And let's hope the twins haven't been brought home there by the police without warning him."

David started the engine and smiled at her. "Thanks, Peter. Feel better for telling you. Let's deal with the twins first, but somehow I don't think they'll be keen on facing your dad without support. They might go to Ingles first and get Aunt Betty to intercede for them . . ."

Mr Sterling, looking very worried, came out with Macbeth to meet them as soon as David drove into the farmyard. Peter was first out of the car, ran over and hugged him, and eased the situation for David by saying, "We've heard about the twins, Dad. We know they're safe because there was news of the explosion in Harkaway on the radio. We came back the moment we heard because we were sure somebody would have told *you*. Do you know where they are now?"

Mr Sterling gently disengaged himself, held his daughter at arm's length and David heard him say quietly, "And has the day gone well for you, my dear?" She nodded emphatically and took his hand as he advanced on David, who was not feeling as cool and collected as he would have liked. "I am glad to know that you are both aware that your brother and sister are safe and uninjured, David. I never listen to the radio at this time of day, but the local police were considerate enough to telephone me at once with the news that Richard and Mary were safe and on their way. They are now with Betty Ingles, who has also telephoned me. I had no objection to them going there first. They were wet and filthy but in good heart, she explained, and were about to be plunged into hot baths. Alfred Ingles and Thomas are out on the hill or in Harkaway, helping with the sheep and searching for casualties. I am not surprised at the calamity in Harkaway . . ." Mr Sterling looked very stern. "The twins have disobeyed my instructions, which were clear enough, and in a sense, David, I must hold you responsible. I am exceedingly displeased."

"But that's not fair, Dad!" Peter said hotly. "How can their disobedience be David's fault? You know what they are. They're not babies and we don't know yet exactly *why* they went up Harkaway. But whatever the reasons, you can't blame David." She went over and stood beside David.

A long silence was broken by Macbeth's excited bark as he dashed to the gate and the twins strolled into the yard. They were clean but rather pale, tousled and subdued. After greeting the rapturous Macbeth, they nodded distantly to David and Peter and went straight to Mr Sterling.

"Sir," said Dickie without his usual confidence. "Dear sir. We wish to apologise for our not doing what you said we mustn't. We are sorry if we have caused inconvenience to all concerned."

A brief silence followed this unusually phrased apology. Mr Sterling opened his mouth to reply but no words came, and then Mary, firmly grasping Dickie's hand, added her confession.

"We are very sorry, but we have often explored that valley in a sort of secret, private way and when we got there I suppose we forgot what you said. *And,* when we were fighting our way up to the top, *and* when all that cruel water was rushing down with dead sheep, I think I remembered what you said – *and* we thought how wise you were. *And* when there is time, perhaps tomorrow, and we're feeling stronger, may we please go back to that private forest to look for our bikes which we left there? At the bottom of the valley by the road."

All that Mr Sterling could do was to nod feebly and mutter something that sounded like "Apology accepted. Very handsome. Thank you, Richard and Mary. Do not disobey me again."

The twins relaxed and turned to smile at their brother. At that moment they heard the telephone ringing in the house. Peter ran in to answer it, but was soon back and looking puzzled.

"It's a man. His voice was vaguely familiar. He asked first if this was Witchend and then for Mr Richard Morton. I asked did he mean Mr David Morton, but he said, 'No, it's Mr Richard I want. The gentleman who witnessed a catastrophe this morning. If he's there, I'd be grateful if he could spare me a few minutes. It's a matter of business'."

"It's *me* he wants," Dickie yelled. "I bet it's James Wilson. He must have heard that bloke Tim doing something on the radio and that's why he knows I'm here . . . Hold on James, I'm coming." And he dashed into the house.

Mr Sterling pressed his hands to his head and tottered after him. Life at Witchend was not what it was!

Mary went over to David. "We are sorry, David, if we've made everything difficult for everybody. It's true that we forgot, because Harkaway, whatever they call it, has been our secret for a long time. Don't be mad with us, 'cos we do like doing things together. We went to see Trudie and the gypsies first. What have you two been doing?"

"Having fun, Mary," Peter smiled. "Don't disobey my dad again, please. He really does know these hills and in his funny way he loves you two very much. Please don't hurt him."

Before Mary could answer, a strange car with a blue lamp on its roof drove into the yard and a man well-known to the Lone Piners got out and smiled at them. His name was Detective-Inspector Cantor. He was short and stout, with a rosy, innocent face, and because he was nearly bald he looked many years older than his actual age. Sometimes he wore spectacles with heavy horn sides, but it was typical of the man that the lenses were of plain glass and the eyes behind them keen and bright. He was much respected by his colleagues and superiors who had nicknamed him "Mister". He had a reputation for courtesy, integrity, and courage, he despised any sort of dishonesty, and was always angered by harm done by criminals to innocent people.

"Hello," he smiled at the three Lone Piners, but before he could say more, Dickie dashed out of the house, saw the police car and recognized the detective.

"Sir," he said breathlessly. "Good afternoon, sir. This is utterly fantastic. I mean, you arriving like this. Do you want to interview us? We could fit you in, but James Wilson of the *Clarion* is on his way here now. I've just granted him an exclusive. I suppose you know we've been involved with the police already this afternoon?"

"That is so," Cantor agreed. "You are Richard, I believe, and I remember that your sister is Mary . . . Yes, Richard, I have come to ask you some questions about your adventure in Harkaway, and I should like Mr Sterling to be with us . . . And Petronella and David Morton, I believe? Of course. We can all talk together."

He shook hands with them and Peter took him into the house to meet her father, who greeted him without much enthusiasm.

"Of course I remember you, Inspector. Please sit down and let us help you if we can. I assume that you wish to question these children about their experience this afternoon. I must tell you that they disobeyed my instructions. This morning, after the storm, I warned them to keep out of the valleys. They have apologized, but from what I hear they only escaped the actual flood by a minute or two. However, they seem none the worse for their experience."

This was not quite true. Peter realized that Mary was near tears and, while Dickie was excited at the prospect of telling his story again, his twin was very unhappy.

Cantor must have sensed this because he dealt gently with her.

"Let me explain why what you saw is so important, Mary. I know you have already told our policewoman that you thought you saw an excited man just above where the hillside collapsed and that after the explosion there was no sign of him. I'm sure you both understand that we must find this man. If he was swept away by the water and was drowned, we must find his body. I know this is horrid for you, but please try to help us. He might be badly hurt. He may be a visitor to the district. A holiday-maker. He may have been with friends who left their car on the Portway. We are making enquiries to see if anyone has disappeared. You see, Richard and Mary, the man in the glider who saw you after the explosion did not see this man beforehand. I know you both well enough to be sure that you are not making up a story and that you think you saw him. Please try again to remember those few seconds . . . Don't interrupt your sister, Richard. We'll hear what you have to say later."

Peter put her arm round Mary's shoulders to encourage Mary, who said, "I've said what I thought I saw lots of times. The more you ask me now, the more difficult it is for me to be certain, but I do think it was a youngish man. He was waving, but I don't think he could see us standing under the tree. We didn't actually hear him shouting, but, although we saw the water burst out, I still think that he might have got off that sort of ledge up there *before* the explosion and that he might not have been washed away. And I'm sure now that he must be a stranger, because anyone who lives round here wouldn't go prancing about up there through the bogs. I can't say any more, Mr Cantor, but he didn't look like a shepherd or anyone we would know..."

"Thank you, Mary," Mr Cantor replied. "We have to find this man if we can. He may be gravely injured. What about Richard?"

"I have to tell our story to Mr Wilson. I've promised, but I won't say anything that Mary hasn't said. She saw the man first and I didn't see as much as she did. I hope you understand, Mr Cantor, but I'm expecting my friend James very soon."

"Of course I do, Richard. I also know James Wilson of the *Clarion*. You may remember we met on the occasion when you caused us some temporary concern by vanishing with a young friend. I believe her name was Harriet?"*

"Yes, sir. That's right. James has just told me that he happened to be in Shrewsbury and heard the broadcast about us and that our adventure might be in the *Clarion* tomorrow. But he didn't tell me why he's up here. I must ask him."

The Inspector smiled and walked over to the window. "I knew he was in these parts as he telephoned me this afternoon. Take Mary and run out and meet him."

* Strangers at Witchend

ENTER MR CANTOR

Then to Mr Sterling he said, "I must apologize for this intrusion, sir, but this is not the first occasion when you and the Morton family have been able to help the police, and the fact is we have another puzzle on our hands. One of the reasons we are interested in what Mary said is that we are faced with a very serious problem and are particularly interested in strangers living in remote parts of the country round here."

Suddenly David was sure that he knew why James Wilson was now in the Midlands. The pieces of the jig-saw began to fit as he turned excitedly to the detective.

"You're lucky again, Inspector. I'm sure we have news for you. Is your serious problem the forgery and circulation of bank notes? Is that why Wilson is in these parts? If it is, we'd better have James in here at once. And the twins, because they really started our interest in your problem. We have something for you, Inspector."

James came in with the excited twins, shook hands first with Mr Sterling and then with the others. "Nice to see you all again, but I didn't expect to meet the Inspector at Witchend. Richard is going to tell me the story of the twins' dramatic escape, but I mustn't interrupt Mr Cantor."

"No reason why you shouldn't stay, Wilson. David was just going to tell me what he knows about forged bank notes in this part of the country. I don't think he is going to waste our time. Mr Sterling understands the situation."

"Mr Sterling does not," the older man said angrily. "He knows nothing about forged bank notes, and does not want this house turned into a police station or a newspaper office. Please be as brief as you can and leave us alone."

Peter went over to her father, sat on the arm of his chair and tried to comfort him.

"We must help him if we can, Dad. Please let David tell what he knows and then James can talk separately to the twins."

Mr Sterling nodded feebly. David glared at the twins and warned them not to interrupt. He then told Mr Cantor of their visit to Bishops Castle market and meeting with Madame Pam, and their belief that they had met this woman before in Rye where she was known as Miss Ballinger and was certainly an artist. James tried to interrupt here, but Cantor signalled silence and David went on to admit how his own suspicions were aroused when, with Peter, he saw Madame Pam himself.

"The first time we saw her was when we first met Jon and Penny Warrender in Rye, and she had with her an attractive young woman called Valerie who she claimed was her niece. This afternoon in Shrewsbury, just as Madame Pam had finished her sketch of Peter, which I bought as a present for Mr Sterling, a young woman rushed up and warned her to pack up because the man the twins saw, as announced on the radio, 'might be *him*'. Mr Cantor, I'm also wondering whether you will be interested to know about Madame Pam. She was an artist before and she still is. Ballinger was very short-sighted and had a hoarse voice. So has Pam. And forgers need artists, don't they? And you have just told me that you're after some forgers. I know you are."

"How?" Cantor snapped.

David told him about their meeting with Jenny in Shrewsbury and of how shopkeepers were being warned. "That's how we know, sir, but there is one more thing. I mentioned our friends the Warrenders just now. They're coming up here soon for Peter's birthday party at the end of next week. They knew the Ballinger better than any of us and I'm sure they would recognize her at once. Maybe I could persuade them to come up here immediately, but even if they do identify her we don't know where she lives."

James interrupted.

"Sorry, Mister, but I must come in here. I know those two youngsters and saw the girl the other day in Rye. As you know, this racket began in the Channel Ports, and I was down

ENTER MR CANTOR

there on business, and now that you're working on it up here I've come to help you."

Mr Sterling began to show signs of stress and Cantor smiled grimly.

"If the woman still goes to markets, we'll soon find her. She only has to be followed to where she's living, but there's no evidence to suggest she's running a forgery racket. If she has a criminal record, her life-style is worth investigation. And even if your young friends do recognized her, that doesn't prove she's a forger. That will need a great deal more evidence."

James agreed. "That is so, but David forgot to mention that when we met in London, and got mixed up in a case of forged pictures there, some woman known as Madame Christabel was running a dress shop on the side. Forgery again, you see. She may not now be actually making the notes, but she may be helping in the distribution. Find her, and she may lead us to the manufacturer."

"True enough," Cantor agreed. "All of you here must now keep out of this business. Specially the twins. The Ballinger or Christabel or Pam must not suspect that she is being watched. Although it might be a good idea for your young friends from Rye to confirm your suspicions, they are not to make themselves obvious to her. You understand this, Richard and Mary?"

"Yes, sir," Dickie said. "But you would like to know where the Ballinger is living, wouldn't you? I mean, if we just happen to find out without her seeing us? We wouldn't even be there, if you see what I mean, but you wouldn't mind us just pursuing our investigations, would you?"

"Probably I would, Richard. David can telephone me if you hear of anything, but you must not go around asking questions of people. You have been helpful, if not very sensible, by not obeying Mr Sterling, but this woman is not to have the slightest suspicion that she is being followed or watched. Understand?"

The twins agreed, but David was left with the suspicion that even now there was something they had not disclosed.

Dickie then took James up to his bedroom for the interview and Mr Cantor left with the promise that he would be in touch the next day. Mr Sterling announced that he was going to stroll up to Ingles and wait until the farmer and Tom got back from helping with the search in Harkaway. Mary said she was tired and would like to go to bed, so Peter went up with her while David made several successful telephone calls, then, as he couldn't find any of the others, went out into the farmyard.

It was dusk, and the bats were fluttering silently round the house. The water in the brook was still higher and noisier than usual, but the evening was very still. Peter came out with the news that Tom had just telephoned to say that he and Uncle Alf were back.

"He says he's too filthy and exhausted to come round now, but that the farmers' search party have found only bodies of sheep and no trace of the mysterious man. I didn't tell him anything about our visitors, David. He's had enough today – and so has Mary. She'll sleep about twelve hours. It's been quite a day, hasn't it?"

David agreed, then said, "Jon and Penny were both at the *Dolphin* and dead keen to come up at once. I didn't tell them too much on the phone. Jon says that unless we hear in the next half hour they'll start very early in the dawn and arrive tomorrow morning. They were thrilled to hear that James has turned up and they seemed to guess why he was up in this part of the world. I've telephoned Trudie to ask if she can put them up at Seven Gates, and like the dear she is she said 'Of course' – till after the party, and how were *you*!"

"What did you say to that?"

"I said marvellous as usual. I can't kiss you now as James is coming."

"That young brother of yours is quite a lad," James

said as he joined them. "He's told a very good story of the explosion and I think I can get it in the paper tomorrow so I must get cracking. You know where I'm staying in Shrewsbury, David. Ring me if you want me or have news. If I'm not about, leave a message for me to ring you." He paused. "Don't quite know how to say it, but don't get too involved in this business. Leave it to Cantor. It's not going to be very pleasant, and all you kids are too nice for this sort of mess."

CHAPTER 10

Not So Clever

Next morning David woke early. Enough had happened yesterday to give him a restless night. He was in love, and had so much wanted the day spent with Peter to be perfect in every way. There had been nothing amiss in their relationship with each other, but he resented the disobedience of the twins, and the intrusion of the Ballinger, and the bringing up again of personalities and events he wanted to forget at this particular time in his life. He liked James, admired Cantor and was fond of Jenny, but didn't want them now unless Peter was directly concerned. As he sat up in bed and pulled back the window curtain, he hoped that they could both even now escape from detectives, journalists and criminals and forget them for a while.

But this was not to be his lucky day. He glanced at his watch. Just after six and the sun was shining and the brook singing down the Witchend valley. Dickie, in the other bed, was asleep and David was determined not to wake him. He grabbed his clothes, crept down to the bathroom and dressed. For a moment he was tempted to wake Peter, but then decided that he wanted to think out things for himself, and to see whether there was any way in which they could escape the consequences of involvement with these other matters. Maybe it would be easier when Jon and Penny arrived, but he'd got to make up his mind now how much he must tell them of what was happening. Perhaps if, and when, the Warrenders had recognized the Ballinger, they could leave matters to the police. Then Penny, now in on the secret of his plans for the birthday celebration, could keep Peter company while Jon helped with some of the planning and the actual arrangements at Seven Gates.

So David wandered out into the sunshine and at once felt better. There was dew on the bracken fronds, which were just beginning to change colour, and as he glanced up at their solitary pine tree he felt strangely moved. Everything began here. How well he remembered the blue-eyed girl with two fair plaits as she rode down one of these beautiful valleys into their lives, and specially into his. All that was best in his life had started here and was now centred in the old house behind him. As he strolled up the narrow path beside the stream, he wondered whether he was taking the Ballinger affair too seriously, and that perhaps when they had talked over everything again he would feel more settled. He stood for a moment to watch a ring ouzel flashing over the stream. Peter had taught him how to recognize the white crescent across the black breast and the piping cry of "Pee-u". And he never forgot afterwards that the few seconds in which he watched the bird were the prelude to the most frightening adventure of his life.

As the bird vanished, he heard, from a little higher up the track, a strangled shout, and looked up to see a bedraggled human figure staggering towards him and waving its arms. The young man was a pitiful sight. Under his beard and moustache his face was deathly pale and streaked with blood. His black jacket and the shirt under it were both in tatters and one leg of his jeans had been torn off at the knee. As David stepped forward to help, the stranger collapsed at his feet and grasped his ankles. David tried to raise him, but he seemed to be hysterical and was babbling words in an unfamiliar language. At last David managed to get his hands under his arms and with a great effort got him to his feet.

The young man did not really understand what he was

saying, but the sound of David's words seemed to bring some comfort and, at last, he made enough effort to keep upright. With one arm round his rescuer's shoulder, he stumbled, a few steps at a time, down the track. He stopped suddenly, as soon as he saw Witchend, then shook his head as he pointed to the house and said something that sounded like "Daw! Daw!"

"Stick it," David gasped. "Nearly home now. You'll soon be OK. Not to worry. We'll look after you."

There was no coherent answer, but as soon as they were in the farmyard, the man stumbled and fell on his face. In panic, David struggled to turn him over. His face was deathly white, and although he was still breathing he was unconscious. David tried to think calmly. Probably this stranger was the young man the twins saw in Harkaway? He was certainly in a dangerous state of exhaustion, probably starving. Should he telephone now for police and ambulance, or was there anything they could do at once? Mr Sterling must be told, but how would he take it? Better wake Peter first. She never panicked and would deal with her father. But not the twins! "Let sleeping twins lie!" David thought grimly as he ran into the house.

Everything was quiet. He tapped on Peter's bedroom door. Not too loudly for fear of waking her father across the landing. There was no reply so he tried again and gently turned the handle. Her window was open and the curtains moving gently in the breeze. Her hair was spread across her pillow and she was still sleeping peacefully. Gently he rested a hand on her shoulder.

"Peter, dear! Pete! Wake up. Help me! Nobody else knows, but there's an unconscious man in the farmyard and I think we should tell your father."

Her blue eyes opened wide.

"David! What *has* happened? Throw me my dressing-gown on the door and go downstairs and wait for me."

That was all. No hysterics. No silly questions and she was down beside him and had given him a quick kiss almost before he had realized what had happened.

He led her into the farmyard. The fugitive was where he had left him, still unconscious. David told her quickly what had happened.

"We must get him to hospital and tell Cantor," he said. "Will you fetch your father at once so we can get this bloke indoors. Peter, darling, he might die on us."

"Right. I'll deal with Dad, but you must telephone now for the ambulance. I don't really know but my guess is that this man is starving. What did he say to you?"

"I just told you. He can't understand English nor speak it. He muttered something which didn't even make sense. While you're upstairs, shall I try to bring him round?"

"No, ambulance first, David. We might do the wrong thing. Dad will know."

And it was extraordinary that Mr Sterling did know. From the moment that Peter woke him with the news that there was an unconscious young man in their farmyard and that David was telephoning for an ambulance, he took control. First the three of them got the man into the kitchen where he soon recovered consciousness, looked vaguely round the strange room and muttered something they could not understand. He seemed to be too exhausted to stand but drank some hot milk hungrily. Mr Sterling searched his few pockets, all of which were empty, and, while Peter did her best to wash his blood-stained face and hands, David went up and explained the situation to the twins, who were furious because they had not been wakened earlier.

"He could be the man Mary saw," David told them. "You can see him when the ambulance comes, but he's in such a state because he's probably been wandering about the Mynd ever since Harkaway. I'm sure he's not English, and I must tell Cantor we've found him. Meanwhile try not to fuss and please do as you're told and help Peter and Mr Sterling. I'm going to telephone now."

"OK then, if you're not bossy." Dickie said. "When you've finished, I wish to telephone James. He must be told of the latest developments. Who is this man, David? It's all rather peculiar and mysterious, isn't it? Did he speak to you?"

"Not really, and I don't think he understands me either. The ambulance will be here soon and he won't be our responsibility any longer. See if you can help Peter, Mary, but don't get in the way in the kitchen."

David then reported to the police. Cantor was not there, but would be informed at once and would probably contact Witchend after he had visited the hospital.

By the time he had finished, Dickie was waiting for the telephone and would not be deterred by the early hour.

"I've got the number of his hotel. James won't mind if I wake him. You don't seem to understand, but finding this bloke and saving his life is what we journalists call 'hot news'. I wouldn't be surprised if James doesn't come rushing over here in his car to take a photo of him. He might take you as well — or instead of, if the other bloke is too ill. I'm James's partner in all this and I don't really mind a picture of you in the paper. Of course, it would be better if you were with Peter and better still if it was only Peter—" and as David tried to grab him he fled into the farmyard.

The kitchen door was shut and Mary outside. "I'm waiting for you, David. I'm scared. I'm sorry for him before I see him."

They went in together. The man was in the chair but still conscious. Mr Sterling, behind him, with a towel in his hand, looked up and smiled.

"His heartbeats are stronger, David, but he's very ill. He may owe his life to you. He has not said anything clearly and does not hear us, but perhaps the hospital can save him . . . I am puzzled by his fingers. See. They are stained yellow as if he has handled acid. This young man is surely no chance visitor to the Mynd. Very strange . . . There is no more we can do for him now, and as we can hardly have breakfast here, perhaps Petronella and Mary would bring us some tea outside in the sunshine."

But before David could get chairs out of the old barn, the ambulance arrived, and five minutes later was on its way to the hospital in Shrewsbury with the semi-conscious man and Mr Sterling's and David's explanations of what had happened.

As the ambulance drove off, Dickie came back, and, after a wary glance at his brother, asked Mr Sterling if he might use the telephone to speak to James. David went into the house with him.

"I know you want to tell James the story and so you shall, I promise," he said. "We'll decide presently what we're going to do today, but remember that Jon and Penny are coming some time this morning. I don't want Pop Sterling bothered any more by the police, nor James for that matter. Pop's done enough, and he gets worried and fussed. If James does come over, I don't want Peter bothered either. We're all here because of her birthday—"

"And you?" Dickie said quietly. "What are *you* going to do today? You're worried about something else, aren't you? Is it the Ballinger? We've forgotten about *her*, haven't we?"

"I wish I had. We don't want her to spoil the next few days. Let's all try and forget her. She's not our business, and I want you and Mary to concentrate on Peter and her party and work in with Jon and Penny when they come. See what I mean? By all means tell James about our visitor, but please go easy, Dickie. We don't all want to get involved."

Dickie nodded doubtfully as he lifted the telephone. David went back to the others, but the truth was that he was unable to practise what he preached. He could not forget the Ballinger, nor the possibility that in some way she was

131

connected with forgery, and he was also very curious about the young man with acid-stained fingers.

They finished their picnic breakfast, and Dickie returned with the news that he had spoken to James who was grateful for the news about the young foreigner and might come over to Witchend later, but would telephone first.

Peter then took David aside and asked him why he was behaving so strangely.

"I know that finding that poor man up our valley was a shock for you, but you did what you could, and nobody could do more. What is worrying you? Even if he dies, it won't be the fault of any of us. I heard Dad say that you may have saved his life, but there isn't anything else that you or any of us can do. It's up to the doctors. What's wrong, David? You're not like the David I know."

David did his best to explain that he wanted them all to get away from, and forget, the events which had crowded on them since they arrived at Witchend.

"Difficult to explain, Pete, but I've got some rather crazy ideas that I want to test out. I'd like to go off in the car for a while to think things out. I don't want your father worried any more, and I'm determined that *you* shan't be either . . . Will you come with me now, darling, just for an hour or two?"

"But why, David? *Why*? What is really on your mind? Anyway, I don't want to leave Dad, and don't think I should. And have you forgotten Jon and Penny?"

"No, but I don't want *them* involved either. Truth is that I want to check up on these ideas and I shan't be able to settle down to anything – specially with you – until I've done this. I know you won't say anything to the others – not even to the Warrenders, if they arrive before I'm back. I understand about you staying here, and in a way I'm glad you are. I'm not sure exactly where I'll be going, but I shall call at Seven Gates – I want a word with Charles. You see, Pete, I'm not only

NOT SO CLEVER

worried about the foreign bloke, but I am seriously wondering whether there can possibly be a link between the Ballinger and the forgery, and this young man. We must have these doubts settled. We don't want Cantor here again. I've told Dickie that I'm not very keen on James coming and raking over all the things we want to forget ... Can't you see, dearest Peter, that it is only *you* who are really important to me? If I can settle the doubts in my mind, I can report to Cantor and let the police get on with it."

Peter stood away from him and put her hands on his shoulders. She was flushed and tears were in her eyes as she said, "I'm a lucky girl, David. You'd better go at once. Will you promise to telephone me from Seven Gates?"

"Yes. I promise to ring you by noon. There's just one other thing. Did you hear that bloke say *anything* useful? Any word at all?"

She shook her head. "No. I just had the idea that he couldn't speak English. You promise, David? To telephone me before noon?"

"Yes, of course. I may be back by then. No need to tell the others why I've gone."

She kissed him quickly and ran indoors. David had nothing to take with him, but as soon as he was up on the Portway he stopped the car, found the Ordnance map which they bought years ago and got out into the sunshine. The view from here was familiar and unforgettable. Away to the west, beyond the Stiperstones, were the blue Welsh hills, and on the other side of the Mynd the long line of Wenlock Edge rose against the skyline. As usual it was very quiet. Here, he was higher than the streams' beginnings, and unless you were familiar with the landscape there was no way of knowing where the heads of the valleys merged into the bogs and heather. David, remembering again the tragic, bemused young man he had rescued only a few hours ago, realized how easy it was for a stranger to get lost in country like this – particularly if he wanted to avoid the only road.

Again he tried to recall the one intelligible word the stranger had mumbled. Something to do with a door? Was he trying to say his name or where he wanted to go?

Inch by inch, David searched the map, looking for a clue. There was nothing on it beginning with 'Daw' that could be the place he hoped to find. Then he spotted a word that gave him a sudden shock of recognition. The lettering was very small, but, sure enough, at the end of a lane branching off the main road which circled the Long Mynd along its western flank, there was a black dot signifying a house called "Appledore". David remembered this house. It had played an important part in their first adventure together when he had first met Peter. It was certainly isolated, and he remembered that Cantor had said that the police were interested in such places. And another possibility was that the Ballinger might be using it now. Did that mean that such a house was used by forgers and that the young man with acid-stained fingers was one of the gang?

Suddenly David felt excited. Now was the time to find out for himself, and then let Cantor take control and get this whole horrible business out of the way. As promised, he could telephone both Peter and the police from Seven Gates. Even if he found nothing outwardly unusual about the place, he could tell the Inspector about his suspicions, and then, thankfully, leave it all to them and concentrate on Peter and her celebration.

So he drove down the steep hill to the east of the gliding station, and turned north until he found a narrow lane overshadowed by trees on the right. This was not signposted, and although he had never before approached Appledore by road from this direction, he turned into it. After about half a mile, it terminated in a rough and rocky clearing, on the side of which a muddy track, once evidently a drive, led up to the house, which was bigger and older than Witchend. David remembered it vaguely, although previously he had approached it by foot from the other side. He got out of the car and looked round. His first suspicion was that the house was empty. There was no sign of life from where he was standing, and a few decaying cabbages in a plot nearer the house suggested that it had not been tended for some time. Then he noticed the marks of car tyres on the track ahead and realized that they were recent.

He was nervous, but had his story ready and decided to take a chance. At least he would soon know whether his surmise about "Appledore" was correct. Then he made his first mistake. He forgot to remove the car's ignition key and left the door unlocked.

David walked up to the house and into a yard at the side where an old estate car was parked. In the back of this he saw several cardboard boxes of greetings cards and realized that his reasoning was correct and that he had found where the Ballinger was living. Then something crunched under his shoes and he saw that the yard was littered with broken glass. He looked up and noticed that a window on the first floor a few feet above the flat roof of an outhouse was smashed. Not just smashed, but broken, probably from inside, because he could see splintered woodwork. Was it possible that somebody had escaped through the window? David's heart thumped excitedly, and as he took a pace towards the shed he heard a girl's cool voice behind him.

"Good morning! You seem to be lost. Have you not realized that this is private property? What do you want?"

She was an attractive young woman, well groomed and wearing nice country clothes. Suddenly David knew that he was right and that he had found the Ballinger's house, and that this was the girl he had seen yesterday in the market, urging Madame Pam to come away at once.

He made his apologies.

"I'm sorry. I'm not meaning to trespass, but I couldn't see anybody about in the front of the house. I believe this is

'Appledore' and somebody told me that an artist called Madame Pam lives here. You see, I met her yesterday in Shrewsbury market and she did a brilliant sketch of my girlfriend. It's her birthday tomorrow and she wants a sketch of *me* and I'm hoping to persuade Madame to give me a few minutes if she's not too busy. If she *is* here, I'd be most grateful if I could see her."

Valerie looked at him appraisingly.

"She does live here. She's my aunt and I help her with her business. You've got a peculiar idea of asking for her at the back of our house. Come round to the front and we'll see if she'll oblige you. It's her day for working at home, but I expect she will. What's your name? Do you live round here?"

"David Morton. My family have a house the other side of the Mynd. Thanks for your help anyway. I know Madame is very quick with her sketches and I would be grateful if she could spare a few minutes. What's you name?"

"Most people call me Val," she smiled over her shoulder. "Come round to the front, David."

He had not expected so friendly a welcome, but as he followed her he remembered that Cantor had reminded him that Madame Pam, even if she was the Ballinger, might be going straight and, in spite of her past record, might not necessarily be a forger. But there was something odd about that broken window.

Val led him straight into a big room on the ground floor crowded with heavy furniture. The hunched figure of Madame Pam was sitting close to the window where the light fell on an easel holding a white card on which she was working.

"Auntie, I've brought you a customer. Name is David Morton who is staying in these parts. You sketched his girlfriend yesterday in Shrewsbury and he wants you to do *him* now. I'm not sure how he discovered where we're living, but he was wandering round the back."

NOT SO CLEVER

"I can't see him from here," she said in her familiar hoarse, deep voice. "Bring him over. I remember a pretty fair girl yesterday . . . Stand close to me, lad. How did you know that I lived here?"

David tried to explain again as he weaved his way between a big table and some enormous chairs towards the grotesque woman by the window. He heard Valerie close the door behind him, and at that moment he began to feel uneasy. Had he really been too clever thinking that he could tackle this sort of situation on his own? True, there were only two women, but had Val tricked him? He looked behind him, but she was only a few steps away and seemed to give him a reassuring smile.

David sat down in the chair indicated by the Ballinger, who took off her specs to peer at him, and then suddenly he realized what a fool he had been. The door was flung back and a man shouted in broken English. "What you two women doing? What the hell goes on here? There is another car. A strange car outside. Fools! Some kids 'ave found Jan. He is in hospital."

David jumped to his feet, stumbled against the easel and fell to the floor. While he was struggling to get up, a second man walked into the room.

"Be quiet, Josef. Who is this young fool and how did he get in here?"

Dazed and trembling, David got to his feet and was foolish enough to make a dash for the still-open door. Seymour, for he was the second man, had little difficulty in tripping him up. David fell again heavily against the corner of the table and lay still on the floor as blood oozed from a cut across his forehead.

Josef swore a foreign oath. Val looked excitedly at Tom Seymour and Madame Pam remarked, "I cannot see clearly what has happened, but when he was close to me I believe that young lout is something to do with those two kids who recognised me the other day."

Seymour nodded, went down on his knees to examine the unconscious David and then turned to Josef and said, "He's out for a bit, but he'll get over it. Carry him down and lock him in the inner machine room . . . And hurry, we may be leaving soon."

Still muttering and swearing, Josef dragged David out of the room, and before he returned Val turned to Seymour. "Is that really true, Tom? That Jan has been found?"

"Yes. Heard it on the car radio. When did that kid get here? Was there anybody with him?"

Val told all she knew and added, "He was interested in that broken window. Why didn't one of you men clear up that mess? It's Josef's job – and it's his fault Jan ran away. Best thing we can hope for is that Jan dies. As soon as he's conscious, he'll split on us, even if he can't speak English. Time we cleared out, isn't it, Tom?"

Josef came back. "I leave him some water. Soon somebody will find this house and so we go. I take what we have made and maybe I burn it some place. We hurry now, Tom . . ."

Then the Ballinger recovered some of her old spirit. "Both you men are responsible for this disaster for allowing that unfortunate young man Jan to join us. Val is right. If Jan lives, sooner or later this house, with the machines, will be found. I also consider you have made a mistake by locking up that boy down below."

Neither man answered to she turned again to Seymour. "No doubt you have made plans to return to one of your hidey-holes in the sunshine. Before we part you will let me know which one, so that Val and I can join you when ready. You will find it difficult to hide from us, and if I have cause I shall betray you, and the police of the world will hunt you down. Now go and pack up. Valerie stays will me and we make our plans now. And do not underestimate me. Madame Pam has been carrying a gun in her handbag since our meeting in Birmingham."

Seymour nodded to Josef and both men went to the door. Then Seymour turned, but Ballinger was too short-sighted to see the meaning look which he gave to Valerie. Neither did she see the girl's answering nod and smile.

CHAPTER 11

Peter to the Rescue

It was difficult for Peter to explain to her father why David had gone off by himself. The morning was only a few hours old, but already enough had happened to upset his gentle and unselfish way of life.

"He's very upset over this young man he found this morning, Dad. Please don't be cross with him. He knows that everything will be all right here with you in charge. He wants to find out where that woman who sketched me in Shrewsbury market yesterday is living. And, I may as well tell you now, that he wants you to have a sketch of him as a surprise. It was his idea. David would have liked me to go with him, but then he realized that you would be left alone with the twins, and then, of course, Jon and Penny may be here soon and I would like to be here when they arrive. David is also going to see Trudie and Charles at Seven Gates about birthday arrangements, I suppose, but he's promised to telephone me by noon . . . So stop worrying, Dad. It's wonderful of you to take all this trouble over my birthday. I'm getting a bit scared of it really, and I'm sorry all these other things keep happening."

Mr Sterling gave her rather a wan but reassuring smile.

"You'll never have another birthday like next week's, Petronella, my dear. I like your friends very much, and have already told you what I think of David, but it is true that when you all get together you are rather overwhelming . . .

Take Richard and Mary out with you now and have a look at Sally. Much as I dislike being disturbed, I will answer the telephone if necessary. Enjoy yourselves in the sunshine."

There was no sign of the twins or Macbeth in the farmyard, but when Peter whistled the Lone Pine call, an answer came from the campsite on the bank above the house. She climbed up to them and sat down and tickled Macbeth behind his grizzled ears. The twins regarded her in silence and Peter was aware that she was not in favour.

"I'm just going to take a look at Sally," she said brightly. "Dad thought you might like to come too. Neither of you have been up on her yet, have you?"

"How very, very kind and considerate of you, Petah," Mary murmured. "I mean, how nice of you to notice that we have actually arrived at Witchend, and are sitting in this solemn meeting-place. Speaking for myself, and without consult from my twin, I would say that I do not wish to visit your pony with you."

"And," Dickie added, "even if we wanted to know where David has gone, and why he has gone, without consult with other members of this Club we do not think we should ask you for the answer."

"Because of negleck," said Mary triumphantly, "shocking negleck. When we remember that it is us who are fighting to keep this Club alive by following its rules, we are thankful in our prayers that other members are on their way here. We shall await their arrival in this ancient place. Do not bother to tell us where our brother has gone."

"Silly little kids," Peter said as she retired gracefully. "I had come to tell you about David, but thank you for looking out for our friends. I'll leave a written message for you if I have to go out. Please don't bother my father with any of your funny antics."

She went then to make a fuss of Sally and was half tempted to go along to Ingles to see Aunt Betty and perhaps have a word with Tom, but decided to stay within reach of the telephone. There was plenty to do in the house, and, although he didn't say much, her father was glad of her company. And she did not feel much like talking because David was constantly in her thoughts. What was it that he really wanted to "sort out" without her? Was he deliberately going into some sort of danger and didn't want her involved? She supposed that she couldn't really blame him for that, but there had never been a time, until today, when he had been so obviously relieved that he was going alone.

Then James Wilson telephoned and she answered, wondering and hoping that it might be David.

"I'm in a hurry, Peter. I'm at the hospital and thought you'd all like to know that, although the bloke David found this morning is now fully conscious, he can't say anything anybody can understand. The doctors won't let anybody near him, but they seem to think he'll pull through . . . Tell Dickie for me that I'll try to come over later and hear what he's got to say. We've got a few lines in this morning's paper . . . All well with you all? Good! . . . See you soon."

When Peter put the receiver down, the twins were at her elbow. Before they could protest, she gave Dickie the message.

"Good about you in the paper! James will bring it for you to see. Go and find my dad and tell him that our patient is a little better. Are you going up to the camp again? We like to know that you're safe and not getting into trouble."

This time Mary have her a wicked grin and said, "It's just that we get a bit bored doing nothing. We were wondering whether we could wander down to the bottom of the Harkaway and see if our bikes are safe. Without or bikes, everything takes so much longer, if you know what we mean? Where's David gone, Peter? We'll never forgive either of you if he's planning something big without us. Are you pining for him?"

She fled as Peter tried to grab her and then the

telephone rang again.

"Hello! Is that you, David darling? I've been longing for you to ring. Are you with Trudie?"

"It's not David darling. It's Jon, Peter darling, and Penny is hopping about on my feet in this hot call-box. Listen, gorgeous. We're about two hours away. Had a puncture and had to change a wheel. Where's David? Has he deserted you?"

"Yes, but not for long, I hope. Sorry about the delay, but we're longing to see you both. Lots of news and some excitement. You'd better come here before you go to Seven Gates. The twins and Dad will be pleased to see you . . . Yes, of course I'll be here. Love to Penny."

When Peter put the receiver down and turned round, she realized that the twins had heard enough of her conversation to know that the Warrenders were delayed.

"*We* shall be here, Peter," Dickie explained. "I am waiting for James and we shall be glad to welcome Jon and Penny and tell them about the Ballinger and that David has gone off by himself."

"There are times, twins, when I long for you to say nothing until you are invited to speak. This is one of them. I know only too well that you are here. My father knows, and I'm sure he will be very angry if you go wandering off again and making trouble for us all. And when Jon and Penny arrive, please don't bother them with your story before we've had a chance to welcome them. James may be here before they arrive, and as he knows them well I don't want you to interrupt."

Dickie looked amazed at such remarks from Peter, but Mary as always was more astute.

"But you're angry with us, Petah. Please don't be. We didn't want to upset you and we're sorry . . . We know you're worried about David going off by himself. We can see that, and if you can't tell us *why* he's gone we can't be worried either. P'raps you don't know why, and of course, that is horrid for you. We'll go back to the camp now and keep out of your way."

And then, of course, Peter was ashamed of herself. She had always understood Mary better than the others and she realized now that the younger girl was hurt by her reproof. And the truth was, she was still disturbed by David's unusual decision. Why could he not be his usual straightforward self and take her into his confidence?

The minutes dragged by slowly. It was now twenty minutes to twelve and he had not telephoned. He had promised and never yet had he broken a promise. Peter went to find her father and told him about Jon and Penny.

"They want to see you, Dad, before they go on to Seven Gates. We could give them something to eat here, couldn't we?"

"Yes, we could. I have been stocking up food for weeks. What about David? Will he be back for lunch?"

"I don't know. He's going to telephone me about now. He's going to see Trudie as I told you. He'll ring soon."

But he didn't. At a quarter past twelve she rang Seven Gates.

"Hullo, Trudie. It's Peter. May I speak to David, please?"

"He's not here, love. Are we to expect him? I know Jon and Penny will be here later, but I guessed they'd come to you first."

"They're on their way, Trudie, but David has gone off alone and he promised to ring me at twelve. Yes, he did, Trudie. He never breaks his promise. Please ask him to ring as soon as he arrives. It's urgent."

"Of course I'll tell him. But what's wrong, Peter? Is your father all right? What are you fussing about?"

"I can't explain over the telephone. There's nothing wrong here. David promised to ring me, and hasn't."

"Well, give him a chance, Peter. He hasn't telephoned here, but no doubt he'll turn up soon. Don't be a silly,

PETER TO THE RESCUE

nervous girl, Peter. Just trust him. You'll hear from him soon."

But she didn't. Another half hour passed slowly before the telephone rang again. Peter had lifted the receiver before Dickie arrived and stood at her elbow, hoping it was James. It was Trudie again.

"Listen calmly, Peter. David has not yet arrived and neither has he telephoned. Fenella is at my side – yes, Fenella. She insists on speaking to Dickie. She is afraid of the telephone, but is very excited and I'm trying to help her. Is Dickie there? If not, please fetch him."

"Of course I'm here," Dickie shouted as he grabbed the telephone. There was a glint in his journalistic eye as he pushed in front of Peter and stood on one leg in excitement. Mary was next to him and Mr Sterling had appeared in the background.

It was quiet in the house. Nobody spoke and they could hear Fenella's high-pitched and nervous message.

"Is that you, Dickie? Really you? I do not like this thing, Dickie, but kind Mrs Sterling has made it work for me. Can you really hear me, Dickie?"

"Yes, Fenella. I am listening and Mary is here. We can both hear you. What do you want to tell me? Don't be frightened."

"I am not frightened now I hear you. It is like a magic. Dickie, tell Mary that I have done what you ask. What you and Mary ask. I will always do what you ask. This is it . . . the house where the fat Pam lives is not far away . . . Some of our Romany friends have told me. It is called Appledore . . . Now I must go, but I always do what you ask and I do not know what else to say—" and then surprisingly and not quite as loud, "I love you both and Petronella very much."

There was a brief, dramatic silence and then the click of the replaced receiver.

Dickie looked round triumphantly, but Peter gave him no chance to speak. Suddenly it was *her* day. Somehow David

HOME TO WITCHEND

must have worked this out about Appledore, and because he did not want her involved he had gone off alone. Just like him. But something must have upset his plans, because he had not got as far as Seven Gates.

"I'm going to Appledore now. On Sally. Dad, please ring the police. Make sure somebody tells Mr Cantor where I've gone and how we found out. James will help when he arrives. Twins, go off to Ingles and try to find Tom and tell him what's happened and that we're not sure where David is . . . And Dad, if David rings, tell him I'm going straight to Appledore, and when Jon and Penny come, one of you twins show Jon the road there. They know the old woman even better than you do . . . Please, Dad, don't worry, because Mr Cantor will look after everything now. And, if there's time, better explain to Trudie."

None of them could do anything with Peter in this mood and nobody tried. As she ran upstairs to put on her jodhpurs, she called over her shoulder to Mary, "Please get Sally for me. Shan't be long."

She was soon ready, but was halfway down the stairs when she remembered her Romany whistle and went back for it. "Darling Romanies", she thought. "They've never let us down".

He father came over to her as she saddled the pony.

"Do nothing foolish, my dear. I have already telephoned the police. Cantor knows by now, but I wish you would go to Seven Gates first. Perhaps Charles will go with you to Appledore?"

Peter swung into the saddle and bent to kiss him. "I'll take care, Dad, but I must find David. He would have telephoned if he could, you know . . ."

The twins opened the farmyard gate for her. "We'll be at Appledore soon," Dickie called. "Not to worry, Peter. Up the Lone Piners!"

But Mary's eyes were brimming as she looked up at Peter and whispered, "Take care and good luck."

PETER TO THE RESCUE

Sally knew every yard of the way up the Witchend Valley to the Portway and loved to be out with her beloved mistress. The noon sun was hot between the hillsides. The stream was still very full and above the sparkling water the shimmering, coloured wings of dragonflies flashed. When they reached the top, Peter heard, as she had always done, the whispering chirp of hundreds of the little brown meadow-pipits as they flickered above the heather and bilberries.

When they reached the Portway and turned south, Peter was reminded again of the stories her father had told her of the ancient men of Britain who had used the same track high above the dangers of the lower slopes and valleys. The view of the Stiperstones and the distant hills of Wales must have looked much the same. It was also strange to realize that in her short life this haunted land had come to mean so much to her. After a while she passed the burnt-out ruins of Beacon Cottage, where only a short time ago they had all shared a momentous adventure and the twins had behaved with great courage.*

Soon after this she turned the pony into a narrower road on the right which led down to the main road. A few hours earlier, David had driven this way, but it was dangerous for cars because there were only a few passing places. The drop on the left was steep and on the right the hillside was almost precipitous. There were several sharp corners and, when she was halfway down, Peter heard, to her horror, the roar of an approaching car ahead. It was coming far too fast and the driver could have had no idea of the dangers of driving at this speed. Peter dare not keep Sally on the road. She could not possibly scramble out of danger up the hillside on the right, so she urged the pony over the edge of the road on her left. Sally was a very sure-footed Welsh mountain pony, and somehow she kept Peter on her back as

* Strangers at Witchend

she slithered to a stop a few yards below the road. Peter slipped off in time to see a big red car take the corner with screaming tyres. She shouted hopelessly in her anger, but she only had a glimpse of the bearded driver with a woman at his side. There was no other passenger and the car vanished before she could take its number.

Peter forgot her own fright as she soothed Sally and eventually urged her up on to the road again. The rest of the journey to Appledore was uneventful. It was years since she had been there, but she remembered that it could be approached by a lane off the main road. She had no clear idea what she was going to do when she got there. It was possible that the couple in the car might have something to do with the mystery. She was sure they were strangers, and possibly they had chosen the route over the Mynd because they wanted to avoid main roads. She was certain, however, that the Madame Pam recognized by the twins and David was not in the car.

But where was David? Had he guessed that Madame Pam was at Appledore? Had their fugitive given him any hint that he had come from there? But David had said that the young man didn't even speak English, and wherever he was now, she was sure that she must first go to the lonely old house they had discovered years ago.

She found the lane and the messy clearing from which she could see the house. She dismounted and noticed that her pony was uneasy. Except for the tracks of tyres in the drying mud which David had seen, there was no other sign of habitation. Then Sally raised her head again and snorted and Peter smelled smoke. Not wood smoke but something like burning oil. Then, above the roof she noticed a wisp of smoke which did not seem to be coming from the actual building. Cautiously she led the pony up the drive, round the side of the house into a sort of courtyard. Here the wrecks of an old estate van and a car were smouldering, and with horror she realized that the burnt-out car was David's. Sally was

PETER TO THE RESCUE

snorting with fright, and for a few endless moments Peter struggled against an overwhelming fear such as she had never known before. "Not *David*," she whispered, and then, as if she was a little girl again, "Dear God, don't let it be David in there."

Sally tugged at her bridle and Peter knew what she must do. She led the pony away and tethered her to a gatepost, and went back as close as she could to the glowing wreckage. There was not a body in either vehicle. Then she saw the broken glass from the smashed window on the first floor. She also tested a back door, which was locked, and as her courage returned she led Sally round to the front of the house again and noticed for the first time that the main door was open. She tethered Sally to a stunted apple tree, and again she felt desperately alone. She remembered the red car with only one passenger and a driver, and she knew that whatever had happened to David he had certainly been here. An open door suggested that whoever was living here had left in a hurry – but where was David?

She must go in through that door and search the house. Courage returned as she remembered that her father and the police knew where she was, and as she stepped forward she heard a muffled thumping noise from within the house. Not unlike the banging of her own heart, she though, as she crossed the threshold into a stone-flagged hall, and with a flash of inspiration whistled loud and clear the call of the peewit which had always been the Lone Piner's signal to each other. There was no answering call, but from somewhere below there came the mysterious thumping. Cellars, Peter thought. There must be cellars. She found the stone steps. The door at the bottom was closed but not locked. She opened it and saw the printing machine. Then from behind the far wall she heard the thumping again – much louder now.

"David!" she shouted, but could not recognise her own voice. "Are you there?"

149

HOME TO WITCHEND

The noise was coming from behind some metal racks holding packs of greetings cards. She tugged at them and they moved towards her. Behind them was another metal door with a key in the lock. She turned the key, the door opened silently and there, with a metal stool in his hands, was David. For a long moment they just stared at each other. Then he dropped the stool with which he had been banging for hours on the door of his prison, and they were in each other's arms. There was a huge purple bruise on his forehead and his face was blood-stained, but after a while they exchanged news in whispers and Peter told him that the front door was open and she believed the house to be empty and she was sure help was on the way. David explained how he had been tricked into the house by Val, how he had seen and recognized the Ballinger, of the arrival of the two men and of how he must have knocked himself out when he fell.

"This is the forgers' secret workshop, Peter. It must be. All this paper on the floor is spoiled bank notes, and here is the printing machine. When I woke up, the light was on and they'd left me water but no food."

Then she told him about his car, but not of her terror that he might have been in it when it was burned.

"I may have left the key in the car. I didn't drive up to the house. I feel better now, though my head feels as big as six footballs. If the others are on their way, let's get out of this dungeon. We must make sure the house is empty."

But it wasn't.

Although feeling sick and very dizzy, David managed the stairs with Peter's help. The front door was still open, but before they went on he said:

"I'd like another look at the big room where I made a fool of myself. I think this is it."

He was in front of her, opened the door and then stepped back in surprise. At the same time they heard a hoarse, deep voice.

"I cannot see you, but you can come in. I am alone."

PETER TO THE RESCUE

At the back of the room near the window, the woman once known as the Ballinger was sitting. Her hands were over her eyes.

"Tell me who you are. They took my spectacles from me. She has deserted me too. There is a lad locked in the cellar below and much else there of interest. I am ready to go now."

And then there was a long silence in the deserted house known as Appledore. David's arm was round Peter's shoulder and he heard her choke back a sob. Ballinger may be an old villain, David thought, but she's going out with courage.

And then they heard the siren of the police car and went out to meet it.

CHAPTER 12

Home to Witchend

The few days that followed the collapse of the Appledore affair passed quickly and happily for the Lone Piners. Inspector Cantor had forbidden any of the young people to approach the house and only James was allowed to witness the removal of the old woman who had been betrayed by the rest of the gang, and deserted by the girl who had worked with her for many years. The police found a loaded gun in her handbag, but the Ballinger made no attempt to use it. Peter and David were closely questioned by Cantor, and a description of the red car, with bearded driver and woman passenger, was immediately broadcast. David confirmed that these two were undoubtedly Seymour and Val, and then did his best to describe Josef, telling Cantor that this man was obviously a foreigner. After the house and cellars had been searched, Peter telephoned her father at Witchend, explained that David's car had been burned, and that he was not too fit and should he go direct to hospital for a check-up.

"Certainly not. Witchend is his home and in his parents' absence I am responsible. Bring him here and I will decide. What are you doing about your pony?"

To her shame, Peter had forgotten about poor Sally, still miserably tethered to the old apple tree and bewildered by what was going on around her. Again her father made the decision. "Telephone Seven Gates and ask Charles and Trudie to drive over and bring with them the gypsy child. She

HOME TO WITCHEND

can ride Sally back there. The gypsies will look after your pony until you can fetch her."

Feeling slightly shaken by this show of authority, Peter did as she was told, having been given permission by the Inspector to ring Seven Gates. Not for the first time she realized that perhaps it would be wise for her to remember that her father was not really such an old man. Just a lonely one, perhaps?

Trudie agreed to come as soon as she had found Fenella, and so Peter brought David home to Witchend in a police car. It was a curious homecoming. The police, with the first aid kit, had done what they could to his bruised face, but he had a bad headache and was very sorry for himself. He dozed with Peter's arm round him on the quick ride back to Witchend.

The twins were waiting in the farmyard, and for once had nothing to say as the driver opened the door for Peter, who helped David out. Dickie took one look at him and rushed indoors, but Mary hugged Peter first and then, rather shyly, put her hand up to her brother's face and touched it gently before flinging her arms round him. Then Mr Sterling came out, followed by Jon and Penny. The driver was thanked, and as he got back into the driving seat turned to Peter and said, "Good luck to you both. Take care of him, love."

David was sent to bath and bed, slept for twelve hours and woke next morning feeling sore but happy. Peter brought him his breakfast and sat on the end of his bed. They were soon joined by Macbeth and the twins, who were strangely subdued. Later, a message came through from Inspector Cantor that a local doctor who often worked for the police was calling to see David, and Mr Sterling refused to let him get up until he had been examined. Jon and Penny arrived before the doctor with the news that they had stayed overnight at Ingles until there was reassuring news about David. Trudie had telephoned to tell Peter that Sally was safe

153

and awaiting her mistress at Seven Gates. She suggested that, until the Morton parents arrived tomorrow, David could use her car, because there was much to be done by the Lone Piners before the great barn was ready for the party.

From then on all went well. David was allowed up. Jon and Penny were escorted by the twins to the Lone Pine camp, but Peter was not allowed to be present as the agenda was secret. James arrived with news and a copy of the previous day's *Clarion* with Dickie's story of the Harkaway explosion. Cantor had intimated that the Ballinger was talking and that their young fugitive was slowly recovering in hospital. It seemed that he was a Czech and that a professor from Birmingham University who could speak his language was now helping the police to get his story. Finally came the news that a scarlet Fiat saloon car had been involved in an accident on the outskirts of Manchester. The driver, a middle-age bearded man, was gravely injured, and a young woman passenger was helping the police with their enquiries.

When the doctor had gone and David was up and about again, Mr Sterling admitted that he had not telephoned Mr and Mrs Morton the previous evening as he did not want them unduly bothered. They were due the following day, bringing with them Harriet Sparrow, the newest Lone Piner who lived in London.

And so the day before the day before the party passed. Jon and Penny drove David and Peter to Seven Gates, where Sally was reunited with her mistress and ridden back to Witchend. David, who had much to discuss with the senior members of the Club, stayed the night there. Tom and Jenny joined them in the evening to make final plans and to hear details of the Appledore adventure.

The next morning, early, David drove to Witchend, picked up Peter and took her to Shrewsbury. They visited one shop together and were on their way back in ten minutes, arriving back at Witchend looking very pleased with

HOME TO WITCHEND

themselves. The twins, laden with two large suitcases, took Peter's place in the car and went on with David to Seven Gates where they retired to the barn with Fenella and set about their scheme of decoration. Penny helped Trudie to prepare bedrooms which were rarely used for visitors. Jenny, with news that she had got three days' holiday, arrived on her bicycle to lend a hand. David and Jon were busy checking lists. Tom arrived with a van from which were unloaded chairs and two long trestle tables. Later in the morning, Charles Sterling and Reuben came in to help and soon the old barn, the second headquarters of the Lone Pine Club, was transformed into what Dickie called "our cheerful and welcoming Banqueting Hall".

The tables were set up in the centre aisle, and at the far end a low stage was built, facing the great white doors. Two of the partitions on each side of the barn were reserved for the caterers who were coming on the day from Shrewsbury. The two redheads, Jenny and Penny, who had not often met, got on well together, but most of the noise came as usual from the twins who, with Fenella, having the time of her life, were trying to fasten home-made paper chains across the banqueting chamber. Dickie and Mary had been working at home on these decorations for several weeks, and but for Fenella's agility and enthusiasm might have been forced to ask for help from their elders. This was avoided, but when they were resting in one of the cubicles with mugs of lemonade, Tom said, "Nice work, kids. Couldn't have done it better myself."

"That is nice for us to know, Thomas," Mary said coldly. "You have always been a great comfort to us. Acksherley our best work is still to come, and if you would kindly find us a step-ladder we will tell you what to do, so that our welcome plan is completed in good time."

Tom was so surprised that he did as he was asked and came back with an excited Jenny as well as the steps. Meanwhile, Dickie had opened the second of their suitcases and produced their home-made offerings – a big, poster-like banner, lettered with loving care with the words MANY HAPPIES AND LOVE TO OUR PETER, and a long strip wide enough to span the barn with the message in the centre in black, bold letters – UP THE LONE PINNERS – and a green pine tree at each end.

"I did Peter's," Mary confessed modestly, "and Dickie did the other which is much more difficult, 'cos it's so long. If we had more time and more paper, we would have liked to do a greeting to Macbeth and Sally."

Tom looked at Jenny, and to his credit made no reference to the spelling of Dickie's message.

"Best ever, twins," he said. "Wish we'd thought of it. Where do you want them to go?"

"Let's hang Mary's 'Happies' where everyone will see it as soon as they come in," Jenny suggested. "Dickie's should go over the stage where David is going to do his big surprise. Come on, twins. Let's use Tom while we've got him."

And so the happy hours passed. In the house, David and Jon were still busy with their lists and the telephone. After a picnic lunch provided by Trudie which everyone – including the gypsies – enjoyed in the barn, another van arrived with a tent which was quickly put up in the farmyard close to the white doors of HQ2.

Then David announced that Peter had just telephoned. "My parents have arrived with Harriet Sparrow and her grandfather and an extra unnamed guest who, I suspect, is not a surprise to the twins . . . All Lone Piners meet at Witchend for final instructions at noon tomorrow, and we then break up to look after our different guests before the party here at seven o'clock. Come on, twins. Charles is driving us home."

Mr and Mrs Morton were waiting to welcome them, and David realized at once that Peter had told them enough of what had happened to reassure them. Before they could ask too many questions, they were joined by Mr Sterling and

Mr Albert Sparrow, whom the Mortons had first known in London where he had an exciting shop selling second-hand books, china, glass, furniture and pictures. Later, they had met him in Yorkshire where he had moved. He always wore rather old-fashioned clothes and the twins privately agreed that, with his thin, spindly legs and a tuft of thinning white hair on the top of his head, he looked rather like his name. He shook hands gravely with them all and then addressed the twins.

"It is a pleasure to see you again, Richard and Mary. I am honoured to be invited here on this most auspicious occasion."

He then shook hands with David and turned towards the house as Peter came out with Harriet Sparrow and a slim boy with straight hair straggling across his forehead and steel spectacles with thick lenses which reminded them of the Ballinger.

"Harry!" Mary shouted. "You've brought Kevin after all. We knew Grandpa Sparrow would help you."

Kevin Smith had met them before and knew Witchend, but he looked shy and bewildered as he muttered, "Hello there, David and twins. You all OK? I brought Brock. He remembered Peter and her Dad . . . Here he is . . . Go find Mackie, Brock."

Brock was an attractive, young, tan dachshund with floppy ears. He was full of the joys of life and pranced forward to greet Macbeth who was a good, but very senior friend.

Harriet was a little older than the twins. An only, rather lonely girl who lived in London. On her first visit to Witchend she had befriended Kevin when he had run away from home and become lost in the hills,[*] and he had never forgotten what her friendship had meant to him at that time.

---

[*] Strangers at Witchend

Next, amid growing excitement, the red mail van drove into the yard and Onnybrook's postman, who had known them all for years, delivered parcels and greetings cards to Peter.

"Not to be opened now," Mary insisted. "All surprises tomorrow. *We'll* look after the parcels." But she laughed when Mr Sterling took them all indoors.

Peter then suggested that the Lone Piners should tidy up the camp, put up two tents with the hope that the juniors, Dickie and Kevin, Mary and Harriet, might sleep out tonight so that there was more room in the house. Although not yet a real Lone Piner, Kevin was accepted as a welcome guest, and several hours passed happily as the camp site under the solitary pine tree was cleared and the tents, each big enough for two sleeping bags, were erected. The camp fire was relaid, and provisions and fresh water in containers brought up in readiness for tomorrow's meeting at noon.

Late in the afternoon, the twins took Harry and Kevin off to Ingles, and David and Peter wandered off on their own. When they came back, they invited Mr and Mrs Morton and Mr Sterling to inspect the camp. Peter's father, of course, was familiar with it, but, although Witchend and the land around it belonged to the Mortons, they had always respected the Lone Piners' privacy and tried not to show surprise at Peter's sudden invitation.

When the adults had recovered their breath and admired the view, Peter took her father's hand and stood with him against the trunk of the old pine tree.

"I feel shy and nervous," she whispered, "but we both want you to see David's birthday present. Everybody will see it tomorrow, but you come first . . . I can't explain how happy I am and how wonderful you are to me . . ."

Then she drew from inside her shirt a thin gold chain on which was threaded her engagement ring.

"David gave me the chain this morning because he says I mustn't wear the ring until the party tomorrow, but I couldn't bear to be without it. Do you like it and do you understand?"

"Clever David," his mother said as she kissed her. "An amethyst to suit your colouring. We think we're very lucky too, Peter darling."

Then Mr Sterling shook hands with David and with Mr and Mrs Morton, but seemed too overcome to say anything beyond, "Very nice, my boy. Most satisfactory."

Mr Morton took Peter's hand and drew her to the edge of the camp where they could look down on the house which meant so much to them all. For a few moments nobody spoke and only the music of the brook broke the silence. Then he said: "You love this place as much as we do, don't you Peter?" And as she nodded because she could not find the words, he added so quietly that only she could hear, "Yes. Home is Witchend, isn't it?"

Not surprisingly, Peter woke early on her birthday morning. So early that there was still a thin veil of mist over the farmyard, and she was wondering whether she should wake David and walk up the valley with him, when there was a gentle knock on her door and her father came in with a tea tray and a pile of letters.

He didn't say much as she sat up in bed and opened her greetings, the most appreciated of which was a coloured sketch of Witchend as seen from HQ1 from Mary, and a miniature booklet from Dickie with a handwrittten description of what his sister had drawn.

"Your parcels are for breakfast time, Petronella, but my birthday gift for you must be opened now." He did not often show any emotion and she had learned not to expect any, but as she took from him a small square package sealed with red wax she realized that he was very moved. Her fingers shook as she broke the wax and stripped the paper wrapping round a leather-covered case. As she opened the lid, he said, "I gave that signet ring to your mother on the day

HOME TO WITCHEND

you were born and have kept it for you until this day."

This was a wonderful prelude to the happiest day of Peter's life, but so much happened that she was never able to remember every event in correct order. More than anything, however, on this golden day she learned the truth and strength of human relationships, of love and loyalty and of gratitude for these qualities. In a way, David was at the centre of everything, but only in a way. He was always about, but he always had been, and anyway she knew now that he was for ever. When she came down, he was in the farmyard arguing with the twins, with Harriet and Kevin in the background. He ran over to her and was the first to give her a birthday kiss, but Mary was close behind.

"Listen, Petah! David stopped us coming up to your room to sing 'Happy Birthday'. You'd better know now that sometimes he tries to bully us. We've got a solemn invite for you. You've got to say yes. You've got to come with us and have a birthday breakfast at the camp. We've got bangers. We want you first today and we don't want David. We've had him all our lives. We just want *you*."

Peter never hesitated.

"Thank you very much, twins, Harry, Kevin, Macbeth and Brock. I should like that. Will you excuse me if I say 'Good morning' first to David's parents?"

And that was another good start to the most perfect of all days. There were presents to look at and cards to pin on the walls of the Mortons' sitting room after breakfast. Then the telephone began to ring and, after a time, Dickie answered it impressively by announcing, "Good morning. This is the Witchend residence," while Mary went to find Peter. James Wilson was an early caller.

"Happy returns and congratulations, Peter. You're my favourite girl but one. Judith is here and sends her love and we shall both see you tonight."

Trudie and Charles rang and so did three girls from the riding stables who chattered in turn for over ten minutes.

Then Tom, with Jenny up behind him, roared into the yard on his motorbike. Jenny was wildly excited and, although Tom didn't say much, he gave Peter a hug that took her breath away and said, "Witchend, Ingles and Seven Gates don't mean much without you, Pete. Have a good day and don't wear yourself out before the party. There'll be plenty of surprises."

The next telephone call was from Peter's uncle Micah and his second wife, Aunt Carol. He had once owned Seven Gates, which was now farmed by his son Charles.

"Your father had told us that today's birthday is very special. It is our intention to join in your merry-making this evening, Petronella, but we send our greetings now."

Jon and Penny were the next visitors, with the news that their respective parents had arrived. "You're going to have quite an evening, you lucky girl! What's that pretty ring on your little finger? We've not seen that before."

"Neither had I until a few hours ago," Peter explained, well aware that this particular ring was not what really interested Penny. Then they gave her their joint present, which was a charm bracelet.

Then Alf and Betty Ingles arrived. As usual, Alf greeted Peter at the top of his voice, and Peter was not surprised when Aunt Betty confessed that she had made the birthday cake which she would see tonight.

Peter was not allowed at the noon meeting of the Club and neither was Kevin, so she took the shy boy up the valley and got to know him better.

Nothing much happened in the afternoon. Jon and Penny up at Seven Gates were with Trudie, supervising final arrangements. The plan, known to them all except Peter, was that after the birthday banquet, when Mr Morton was going to propose her health, David was going to welcome and introduce old friends and acquaintances of the Lone Piners to the Birthday Girl. It was this plan that had given him so much work during the past few weeks, though he had been helped by Jon and Penny.

The first guests arrived just before seven o'clock, and none of them recognized the old barn in its party dress. Only this morning Charles had decided that it must be lit by electricity and not by the usual oil hurricane lamps and had called in lighting experts from Shrewsbury. Now there were lamps down the long table, fairy lights suspended from the roof and spotlights focused on the big doors and on David's stage at the opposite end.

At one time it had been suggested that Peter and her father should welcome the guests at the doors, but both firmly declined. Although the final result was crowded, chaotic, informal and noisy, it was very happy. The Mortons, Peter and her father arrived first, closely followed by the Ingles who had collected Mr Sparrow, Harriet and Kevin.

Peter, Jenny and Penny had already agreed to wear long dresses, but when Mary discovered that Harriet did not have one, not even her mother could persuade her to wear hers. The boys – even Tom – wore suits and all looked uncomfortable and rather tense. Peter, of course, was in blue, Jenny in her favourite green and Penny, the other redhead, chose deep cream.

As David urged the Lone Piners into the barn, Mary whispered something to Dickie and ran across the yard to the Romany caravan. He hesitated for a moment, then nodded, joining the others now gathered round Peter and taking charge of Harriet, who refused to leave Kevin. Tom and Jenny, standing close to each other, were rather quiet, but in a few minutes, as the guests pressed forward to greet Peter, the reception which David had planned was even more successful than he had hoped. Jenny's father and stepmother arrived, followed by Penny's parents and Jon's mother from Rye. Then Peter's bearded Uncle Micah, looking like an Old Testament prophet, arrived with Aunt Carol. They were followed by his son Charles and the beloved Trudie who had done so much for the Lone Piners. Next, James Wilson with his gorgeous wife Judith, who laughed as her husband embraced both Peter and Penny. As the adults took their places at the tables, Mary came back with Fenella, who looked superb in a coloured gypsy dress. She was dumb with shyness and blushed scarlet when Peter stooped to kiss her. Then Trudie slipped out for a few moments and returned with Reuben and Miranda, both in traditional dress. Mr and Mrs Morton went over to greet them and then Miranda went to Peter, kissed her and whispered a few words that nobody else could hear. Peter smiled and nodded, and David, at her side, heard her say softly, "I'm wearing your whistle, Miranda, just in case you didn't come."

At last the guests were seated. The Lone Piners and their parents were at the top end of the table and, as Dickie confirmed later, "It was a fabulous feast considering everything was cold, but, of course, there was plenty of sparkling drink and Aunt Betty's enormous cake, but nobody seemed very hungry or thirsty. Funny peculiar really."

Presently, Mr Morton stood up and banged on the table. He spoke simply. Said that he had been asked by Peter's father to ask them all to drink to Peter's health on her important birthday.

"Since we have known her," he went on, "we have all loved her, and so, I am sure, does everybody here. And now I would like to say a little about her closest friends who, as usual, are grouped round her now. We know they are called the Lone Piners, and we know that the most important of their rules is to be true to each other whatever happens always – not a bad rule for us all in these days. When we have drunk our birthday toast to Peter, perhaps somebody else would like to propose one to the Lone Piners which I think should be coupled with words particularly suited to them. They are 'From Loyalty to Love'. I have always thought their behaviour and respect for each other and to those of us who are older are an example to us all."

A burst of applause interrupted him and then he added, "David has something important to say to us in a moment, but first let us drink a birthday toast to Petronella. Congratulations and happy birthday, dearest Peter."

They stood, lifted their glasses, drank and cheered and the twins' treble voices were the first to lead them all in "Happy Birthday to You".

Then Mr Morton nodded to David who whispered to Peter and then stood up. In the sudden silence he too seemed dumb. He glanced across at his mother who smiled and nodded; then Jon called "Speak up, David. We're all waiting."

David gulped and found the few words he wanted. "Only thank you. Thank you to my father. Thank you from Peter and me to you all for coming. I have nothing else to say but something to show you—"

There was not a sound as he took Peter's hand in his, and as she stood beside him he took from his pocket the amethyst ring and slipped it on the third finger of her left hand. She was not shy now and stood proudly by him as the cheers broke out. Mr Morton stood up again.

"I want you all to know that David will now be studying and working with solicitors in Shrewsbury and so will be often at Witchend. And then one day, when these two are ready, our gift to them both will be the house we all love. I told them yesterday that their home is Witchend."

More applause, as Peter, with tears she could not check and words she could not say, kissed both Mr and Mrs Morton, but before she could sit down, Tom jumped up and shouted, "Good luck to them both, Jen and I say, and so say all of us. We've got a surprise too. Look what *my* girl's got." And he stooped and lifted Jenny easily to stand on a chair beside him. "Show them, Jen," he grinned as she raised her left hand to show them all a gleaming emerald ring. Applause again, and Peter was the first to hug her as she whispered, "We hope you don't mind, Peter. Only Mum and Dad and

Uncle Alf and Aunt Betty knew. Tom wanted it this way because you come first with us."

Then the toast to the Lone Piners and "From Loyalty to Love" was drunk, and Peter, with an eager twin on each side of her, cut the first slices from her gigantic cake, and Dickie shouted, "First slice for Aunt Betty who made this monerment. Cheers for the best cook in all Shropshire."

"And our love to her," added Mary.

Then the boys moved the table back against the wall and David stood on his little stage and called for silence.

"We've arranged a special surprise for Peter. We hope she hasn't guessed, but most of you have helped to make it work. Outside, in that tent, are a few friends that the Club has made since Peter founded it. Not all those we asked have been able to come, but we are grateful to those who are waiting now to greet Peter and her friends again. When we have welcomed them all, our old friend Reuben is going to play his accordion for us so that we can sing and dance. Jon will announce them ... Who is first?"

"Detective Inspector Charles Cantor," Jon announced. "Known to all his friends and some of his enemies as 'Mister'."

Those guests who had never seen him before were amazed to see Mister's rosy benign face and innocent smile as he walked, with a twin on each side, to greet Peter. Nobody heard what he said to her, but she laughed and dropped him a mock curtsey. Then, after shaking hands with Tom and Jenny, he turned to David and said quietly, "Good luck to you both, lad. No need to tell the others now, but thanks to your description of the man Josef we have him. The booking clerk at Shrewsbury station didn't like the look of the twenty pound note he offered for a ticket to London."

The next surprise guest was a frail, white-haired old lady, who walked in with the help of a stick. Jon announced her as "Mrs Agnes Braid, once of Witchend and now retired to Clun." Mr and Mrs Morton and the twins rushed to meet their old friend and housekeeper who had once looked after the house for them while they were in London.

Then came a confident, cheerful young man not much older than David, whom they had first met in Devon. "Dan Sturt, journalist," Jon announced. "He won't let me call *him* Mister." Dan laughed and almost ran to greet Peter, took her hands and kissed her before she could protest. "David remembered," some of them heard him say. "I told you to ask me to your engagement party. Good luck to you both, and come to Devon for your honeymoon. Where's that redheaded friend of yours?"

Next was Nicholas Whiteflower, a fair-haired boy a year or two older than the twins, who ran to meet him. "Nicholas is our idea," Dickie shouted. "We lost him for a long time, but David helped to find him." Jenny detached herself from Tom and joined them because she had been the first Lone Piner to befriend Nicholas, and after he had shyly spoken to Peter she kept him at her side with Tom.

Then came the bachelor Alan Denton, sheep-farmer from Clun, who had met Jon and Penny in a train when they were on their way to Shropshire where they first met Peter on the adventure that followed.

Next was Peter's greatest surprise and she never knew how David had found him.

"Herr Johann Schmidt, better known as John Smith. Although his home is in Germany, he too knows the Shropshire hills," Jon announced.

This extremely handsome young man seemed completely at ease. He bowed courteously to the guests, most of whom were rather taken aback by this stranger. He went straight to Peter, took her hand and kissed it, then shook hands with David. He said in perfect English, "I am honoured to be here. I have never forgotten what you did for me, and never have I doubted that you were for each other."

"We've never forgotten you either, John. Thank you for coming. I remember that when you went you said, *'Auf Wiedersehen'* and I know that means 'Till we meet again'."

John was the last of the special guests and, as Peter and David stepped down to introduce them to each other, Dickie, who had been whispering to his father, jumped up in their place with Mary beside him. Mr Morton called for silence again and Dickie made his first public speech.

"Everybody is getting too old and busy for the famous Club of ours. There's grown-ups here who know what we can do. Mary and me and Harry want everybody to know that this Club, which isn't as secret as it was, is going on just the same and better. Kevin is our next member, and when all this fuss is over he is going to sign our oath in blood on the old dokkerment which we dug up from under our Lone Pine tree this very day and it says to be true to each other whatever happens always—"

Here, almost overcome by emotion and loss of breath, Dickie gulped and wiped his forehead and Mary took this opportunity to add, "And don't you older ones forget that, although you will always be welcome, Nicholas over there is going to have an invite, although he doesn't know it, and so is Fenella, and as Mackie is getting rather elderly we'd better have Kevin's Brock—"

Then amidst cheers, Tom stood up beside them and shouted, "The Club would be nothing without 'em. Good luck to the young 'uns."

Cheers again and glasses raised as Mr Morton pointed to Dickie's banner and they all drank to the toast of "The Lone Piners".

And that is nearly the end of the story, but before the party broke up, David managed to get Peter away from the others and out into the moonlit farmyard. As he drew her into the shadows and held her close, she whispered, "Thank you, David, for the most wonderful evening of my life."

"Something special I wanted to ask you, Peter. What

did Miranda whisper to you?"

"She asked me whether a promise she made to me, more than once, had now come true."

"And what was that?"

"That I should find my heart's desire. And I have, David." She smiled at him. "Could we go home now?"

"Yes. Let's do that. Home to Witchend."

Appendix

The Lone Piners, their relations, friends and enemies featured in this story have also played a part in the following books:

PETRONELLA ('PETER') STERLING
Mystery at Witchend, Seven White Gates, The Secret of Grey Walls, Lone Pine Five, The Neglected Mountain, Saucers Over The Moor, Wings Over Witchend, The Secret of the Gorge, Mystery Mine, Not Scarlet But Gold, Man With Three Fingers, Rye Royal, Strangers at Witchend, Where's My Girl?

DAVID JOHN MORTON
Has appeared in every Lone Pine story.

RICHARD AND MARY MORTON
The twins have appeared in every Lone Pine story.

THOMAS (TOM) INGLES
Mystery at Witchend, Seven White Gates, The Secret of Grey Walls, Lone Pine Five, The Neglected Mountain, Wings Over Witchend, The Secret of the Gorge, Not Scarlet But Gold, Man With Three Fingers, Strangers at Witchend, Where's My Girl?

JENNY HARMAN
Seven White Gates, The Secret of Grey Walls, Lone Pine Five, The Neglected Mountain, Wings Over Witchend, The Secret of the Gorge, Not Scarlet But Gold, Man With Three Fingers, Strangers at Witchend, Where's My Girl?

JONATHAN (JON) PETER WARRENDER
The Gay Dolphin Adventure, The Secret of Grey Walls, The Elusive Grasshopper, Saucers Over The Moor, Lone Pine London, Mystery Mine, Treasure at Amorys, Rye Royal.

PENELOPE (PENNY) WARRENDER
The Gay Dolphin Adventure, The Secret of Grey Walls, The Elusive Grasshopper, Saucers Over The Moor, Lone Pine London, Mystery Mine, Treasure at Amorys, Rye Royal.

HARRIET SPARROW
Lone Pine London, Mystery Mine, Not Scarlet But Gold, Strangers at Witchend.

ALBERT SPARROW (Harriet's Grandfather)
Lone Pine London, Mystery Mine, Strangers at Witchend.

MISS E M BALLINGER (Also known as Madame Christabel, Miss Emma Cartwright, Mrs Louis Sandford and Miss Saunders)
The Gay Dolphin Adventure, The Elusive Grasshopper, Lone Pine London, Treasure at Amorys.

THOMAS SEYMOUR (Also known as 'Slinky Grandon' and Mr Phillips)
    The Gay Dolphin Adventure, The Elusive Grasshopper, Lone Pine London.

VALERIE (Sometimes known as the Ballinger's niece and ocne as Dorothy Smith)
    The Gay Dolphin Adventure, The Elusive Grasshopper, Lone Pine London, Treasure at Amorys.

DETECTIVE INSPECTOR CHARLES CANTOR (usually known as MISTER CANTOR)
    The Secret of Grey Walls, The Neglected Mountain, Man With Three Fingers, Strangers at Witchend.

JAMES WILSON
    The Elusive Grasshopper, Lone Pine London, Sea Witch Comes Home, Rye Royal, Strangers at Witchend.

DAN STURT
    Saucers Over The Moor, Where's My Girl?

ALAN DENTON
    The Secret of Grey Walls, The Neglected Mountain.

NICHOLAS WHITEFLOWER
    The Secret of the Gorge

JOHANN SCHMIDT (Known as John Smith)
    Not Scarlet But Gold.

KEVIN SMITH
    Strangers at Witchend.

REUBEN, MIRANDA and FENELLA
 Seven White Gates, The Secret of Grey Walls, Lone Pine Five, The Neglected Mountain, The Secret of the Gorge.

AGNES BRAID
 Mystery at Witchend, Seven White Gates, The Secret of Grey Walls, Lone Pine Five, Wings Over Witchend..

The publishers hope that you have enjoyed this story and would like to know what you think of it. You can write to them and they will answer your letter, which should be addressed to:

Jade Publishers
10 Mandeville Road
Aylesbury
Buckinghamshire
HP21 8AA

The story you have just finished is one of the adventures of the members of the Lone Pine Club. Each adventure is complete in itself and there are now twenty of them. The complete list is as follows:

1. MYSTERY AT WITCHEND
2. SEVEN WHITE GATES
3. THE GAY DOLPHIN ADVENTURE
4. THE SECRET OF GREY WALLS
5. LONE PINE FIVE
6. THE ELUSIVE GRASSHOPPER
7. THE NEGLECTED MOUNTAIN
8. SAUCERS OVER THE MOOR
9. WINGS OVER WITCHEND
10. LONE PINE LONDON
11. THE SECRET OF THE GORGE
12. MYSTERY MINE
13. SEA WITCH COMES HOME
14. NOT SCARLET BUT GOLD
15. TREASURE AT AMORYS
16. MAN WITH THREE FINGERS
17. RYE ROYAL
18. STRANGERS AT WITCHEND
19. WHERE'S MY GIRL?
20. HOME TO WITCHEND